G000136884

Beyond Love and Hate

The Wardham Series
Book No. 4

ZOE YORK

Copyright © 2015 Zoe York

All rights reserved.

ISBN-13: 978-1-926527-12-3
ISBN-10: 1-926527-12-7

OTHER WORKS BY THIS AUTHOR

DEDICATION

unexpected pleasures are such a wonder

For my Wardham Ambassadors

CHAPTER ONE

Perched on a craggy point jutting proudly into Lake Erie, Go West Winery was Beth Stewart's pride and joy. She'd been the first non-family, non-friend the West brothers hired five years earlier, and as of two months ago, had been promoted from Marketing Manager to Director of Operations and Guest Services.

So why was she about to paste on a fake smile and take a meeting with the insufferable Finn Howard? Because the monster had scared away her replacement, and now she was left wearing both hats, two weeks before the Essex County Toast to Summer Wine Festival. The event was the biggest opportunity of the season to cement their brand with wine fans flooding in from all points between Detroit and Toronto. And advocating for the changes that would benefit Go West meant clashing with the sexy, bossy, completely unlikeable marketing officer from the growers' association.

Right on cue, the devil arrived, his high-end sedan that didn't impress her in the least purring to a silent stop in Evan's parking slot. Of course he would ignore the polite "Reserved" sign. As he stepped out of the car, pausing to adjust his suit jacket, she braced herself against the visceral pulse of pleasure she'd come to expect each time they met.

She was pathetic, lusting after a man she didn't like. Could barely stand to be in the same room as, yet wanted desperately to get naked with. Because Finn Howard naked? That would impress her. Striding toward her in a dark grey suit, light blue shirt and black tie, he made her weak at the knees. Naked, she'd probably faint.

Of course, that would never happen. For one thing, if Finn was naked, she'd probably be naked, too, and there was no way she'd give Mr. Perfect a glimpse of her four-years-on-the-wrong-side-of-thirty thighs or her soft, doughy tummy.

Which just made her hate him even more, that he rendered her speechless and self-loathing, when normally she liked her curves and knew how to pair them with a saucy look and a teasing smile. With any other man, Beth had confidence to spare.

But this man was the devil. Time to armour up.

She lifted her voice, willing it to be strong and just loud enough to compete with the late spring wind. "Careful, Mr. Howard. Rumour has it the Director of Operations has employed the services of a towing company to ensure that reserved spots are, in fact, reserved."

He paused, and for a second she thought he might smile, but after a frozen beat he resumed his steady pace in her direction.

As he drew abreast, he murmured, "Just remember not to screech, okay?"

Screech? Was that something she did on a regular basis? No, it wasn't. She could feel her eyes flashing wide and crazy-like as she spun to follow him inside. But damn him, now she felt like screeching. Stomping her feet and having a tantrum sounded good, too, and their meeting hadn't even begun. Fan-fucking-tastic.

"Are we in the boardroom today?" He asked the question blandly, as if he hadn't just insulted her. And she still didn't understand what the insult had meant...why was she going to lose her mind?

"No, I've got everything in my office."

He nodded in agreement, and stepped out of her way so she could mount the staircase ahead of him. With each step, she silently repeated her goals for the meeting.

1. Get buy-in for more prominent Go West brand placement

2. Don't imagine him in his underwear

All she had to do was stay focused on those goals. Be professional. And, apparently, not screech.

As she settled behind her desk, she kept her attention squarely on the papers in front of her. The map of the Kingsville Country Club covered in Post It notes indicating stall placement. Finn's original plan in yellow, her changes in green. She took a deep breath and willed herself to stick to the indisputable facts—

"Great, I see you've arrived!" Ty West jogged into her office, his shirt-sleeves rolled up past his elbows. He'd probably just come from downstairs, where he belonged. Beth shot him a puzzled look that he totally missed. "Sorry Evan couldn't make it, but he ended up having to take the first train to Toronto this morning. Don't know how the guy does it. Anyway, have you told Beth the good news?"

"What news?" She left off the word good because she doubted it would actually apply, given that Finn had been nothing but a thorn in her side for the last year. She'd shared her concerns with the West brothers more than once but Ty didn't care about marketing at all and Evan was thinking bigger than the local market. That left her holding the bag. And all the problems Finn put in it.

Across the desk, her nemesis cleared his throat. "Not yet, I thought she'd probably want to hear it from Evan."

"Too bad, so sad. Big brother has a meeting with some Japanese buyers today, so it's up to us to welcome you to the family."

Welcome to the— "No." Finn raised one eyebrow in her direction. She didn't care. It hadn't come out as a screech. Her protest was calm, cool and collected. And definitive, but in case there was any confusion… "I mean, hell no. Did someone offer this man a job without consulting me? Because I'm pretty sure I'm in charge of that type of thing now, and he is a terrible candidate to work for Go West Winery."

He grinned. "Good thing I'm not going to be an

employee, then."

"Oh, thank god." Beth turned to Ty, who stifled a laugh. "What?"

"Finn's agreed to come in as a marketing consultant for the summer."

The devil leaned back in his chair and winked—winked!—at her. "See? Consultant." He pulled the syllables out, long and slow, as if big words might be a challenge for her.

"Actually, it wasn't so much agree…more like suggest, is how Evan tells it." Ty shrugged. "Seemed like a good idea to me."

Something tickled at the back of Beth's throat. Something hard and dry like pure embarrassment coated in shards of glass. Once she started coughing, she couldn't stop. Before she realized he'd even moved, Finn was around the desk and kneeling in front of her, holding a bottle of water. "Here," he muttered dryly. "If I knew stifling the screech would have been so difficult, I wouldn't have warned you."

"You…you…you…" Words failing to squeak past the catch in her throat, she accepted the water and took a few sips. Vocal ability restored, she shook her head. "You suggested this? Why? We don't work well together. No offense." She grimaced. "Okay, that sounds offensive. But—"

He shifted back on his heels. Up close, his grey eyes had flecks of blue in them, and his perfect white teeth were slightly crooked, which just made him more interesting. No grey in his thick black hair, but maybe he dyed it. Ha. As if. And his gaze had a hint of something that looked like affection in it. "We don't get along, I grant you that. But I think we work well together. The end result is always spectacular."

"You can't be a consultant for us—you work for the growers' association. It's a conflict of interest, and in a way, we'd be paying you twice." All of a sudden aware of his proximity to the bare skin of her calves, Beth twisted in her chair and tucked her legs under her desk. Why did she wear a skirt today?

Stupid question. She knew why. She wasn't proud of it, either.

"I've done projects for other member wineries before. I can wear multiple hats." His voice was low and far too smooth for her liking. He'd practiced this conversation and had the advantage.

As if he thought she was about to narrow her gaze and spew venom at him—and frankly, he wouldn't be far off from the truth if she didn't rein it in—he pushed effortlessly to his feet.

Don't stare at his thighs. Don't think about what the muscles pressing against the front of his pants would look like naked. Definitely don't follow the obvious path north--

"Beth?"

She jerked her attention back to Ty.

"We good here?" He shoved his rolled up shirt sleeves higher on his corded arms and propped his hands on his narrow hips, emphasizing the length and breadth of his v-shaped torso. Ty had a certain charm, or so thought all the women in Essex County. Why couldn't she have a stupid crush on her handsome boss whose only fault was being selfish? Instead she was stuck salivating after the even more handsome and much more cruel Finn Howard.

But a crush was not an excuse to be unprofessional. "We're good. Finn and I need to hammer out some boundaries, but we'll make this work."

A pregnant pause filled the room as Ty left, then Finn took a deep breath and clapped his hands together. "Are you really going to be okay with this?"

"I'm going to have to be. You scared off my replacement and I don't have time to hire and train someone new before we're in the thick of event season."

"I do have some usefulness, you know."

She shrugged. "Probably."

That earned a chuckle, although she somehow felt he wasn't laughing with her. "I suppose we should discuss the parameters of my role."

"Of course." She squared her shoulders and pinned him with what she hoped was a sufficiently frosty look. "You're a consultant. You'll provide your expert opinion, and I'll make the final decisions. I can handle that as long as you remember who's in charge."

He gave her a careful, assessing look before returning the shrug. "Sure."

Could he be any more dismissive? Beth took a deep breath to settle her nerves. "Fine. Your first job as a consultant is to figure out a way to increase our visibility at Toast to Summer."

"Go West has the largest logo on all the marketing material, do you really think your visibility is lacking?"

"Our visibility, Finn. Got that? And I'm talking about visibility on the ground. Here are my proposed changes. Can you make them happen?" She pushed her prepared notes toward him. He picked them up and made a non-committal grunting noise. She tamped down the instinct to snap at him and settled back in her chair. Waiting was a power strategy she'd learned from Evan. It worked.

"I'll need to fire up my laptop and make some calls. Give me half an hour." Finn shoved away from her desk with a start. "Anything else, boss?"

"Let's see how far you get with that first."

"You got it. I'll get out of your hair and go work in the boardroom."

— —

It only took him five minutes to convince the coordinator from Winding Path to switch stalls with Go West. Finn knew how to sell what he wanted sold. The next twenty-five minutes were spent chewing over what the hell he was doing down the hall from Beth Stewart.

He shoved one hand through his hair. The woman drove him mental, and it wasn't a mystery why. She was gorgeous, lush and curvy with full pink lips that drove him to distraction. Her voice heated his blood and her touch, on the rare occasions he experienced it, stole all thoughts from his head.

She was perfect. And totally off-limits. Beth was the marrying kind of woman, and Finn had no intention of ever getting hitched.

Right on cue, his phone beeped. A text message from Janine. Can you take the boys to McDonald's for an hour tonight?

He sighed, hating himself for his first response. He didn't see them that often. It was the least he could do. He tapped back a quick confirmation and glanced at his watch. He'd planned on working on proposals all evening. Now his night was going to be sticky fingers and hamburger grease, fart jokes and an awkward conversation when he dropped them off. She's doing the best she can right now. She didn't ask to be a single mom with four kids under the age of ten.

He could kill his brother-in-law on days like today. Ex-brother-in-law. Jackass had moved to Northern Alberta for work and ended up shacking up with a new family. Leaving Finn holding a bag he'd never wanted in the first place.

He'd watched his parents struggle to raise five kids in a three-bedroom bungalow. All of his siblings had followed a similar path, even his youngest sister Kath who was pregnant with her first child at twenty-three.

Not for the first time, Finn wondered if he'd been adopted. If he didn't share the same dark hair and grey eyes as the rest of his siblings and his father, he'd have been sure of it.

At least his brother Ryan didn't live in the same three-block radius as the rest of them. He'd moved up north. But he was still juggling two jobs, three kids, and a wife who seemed more trouble than she was worth.

And Finn was going to McDonald's with his sister's kids.

Shit. Thirty-eight years old and having a Happy Meal for dinner.

He shoved his stuff in his briefcase, grabbed Beth's floor plans, and headed back to her office. She was concentrating on something, nibbling on her lower lip while she read her computer screen, and he paused in the doorway. He did this sometimes, watched her when she wasn't paying attention. She worked with deliberate efficiency, planning ahead to avoid costly errors. Her conservative nature meant he needed to push her out of her box from time to time, but it hadn't been a surprise when the Wests promoted her. She was a natural manager.

The constant tug of arousal pulled him into her space. His determination not to act on it made him scowl. She glanced up, and the combination was not well received.

"Run into problems already?"

He couldn't help but grin. She wasn't bitchy with anyone else, and that made him think it was because he got under her skin. And he was just enough of an asshole to like that even if it couldn't go anywhere. "Not at all. Here are your changes, just as you requested. I'm heading out now, I'll be back tomorrow."

She arched one brow. "Short day."

"Something came up." They were six and eight and loved french fries and ketchup served in equal proportions. He'd probably take them to the park to burn off that crap afterward.

"This needs to be a priority, Finn. If you can't make time…" She sighed and reached for the floor plan, apparently thinking twice about finishing that sentence. "Thank you. When will you be back?"

"I'll start on the marketing plan tomorrow." His jaw twitched, wanting to say more, unsure which words would thaw her frost towards him. Uncomfortable with why it mattered so much to him. Before he could dwell on any of that, his phone rang. He twisted away from Beth's sharp gaze and answered. His mother wanted to know if he'd bring the boys there instead of going out.

If you're free, why am I watching them? He hated how he jumped straight to resentment. Jesus, he needed a vacation. "How about after dinner instead? I'm at Go West today. Should I bring a bottle of wine?" Chiding filled his ear. He knew his father only liked beer, why antagonize the man? Maybe because I work in the wine industry and he might try being proud of that for a change? "Fine, I'll pick up a six-pack. See you then."

He turned back to say goodbye to Beth, but she'd turned back to her computer screen. He wasn't up for another battle. Probably for the best, even if it did flood his gut with disappointment.

CHAPTER TWO

It was a twenty-five minute drive from the city to the winery and the entire way he kept glancing at the twin Starbucks cups in his centre console. It wasn't like he'd never bought a woman coffee before. But usually when he did, it was with a reasonable degree of certainty that she'd appreciate the gesture.

He pulled into the parking lot. It was tempting to nab Evan's spot again as he had the day before, but the agenda for today was peacekeeping. Even though he knew the company president was out of town for the week, he didn't want to antagonize Beth—much. God, he loved the flare in her eyes right before she snapped at him. Her bark had zero bite, although the thought of Beth biting him…that worked too.

He slipped his laptop bag strap across his body and headed inside, where he found Beth waiting at the top of the landing, holding two takeout coffee cups of her own.

She started to laugh. "Great minds, eh?"

"What did you get me?"

She gave him a funny look. "Black Americano. That's right, isn't it?"

Jesus, he was so fucked. Warmth filled his chest and wiggled its way down to the dick. "Yeah." She turned and he admired the flare of her ass. Today's skirt was snug to mid-thigh, then flared, and with each step he caught a glimpse of bare thigh. Totally, completely fucked. He needed to do something about this crush—it was getting out of hand.

"Sorry about leaving early yesterday," he muttered as

they set their four coffee cups together in the centre of her desk.

"You're here early today, that's all that matters." She pasted on a bright smile, and he decided not to try to and read anything beyond what she was showing him. Moving on. "What do you need to get started?"

He cleared his throat. "Budgets and marketing calendars from previous years if you have them."

She handed over a USB stick and a thick binder. "I've got a staff meeting at nine, but I'll be around before and after that."

"Could we have lunch?" He blurted out the invitation and immediately wanted to take it back.

She arched one brow in surprise. "Lunch?"

Yeah, good question. "A working meal, of course. I want to know more about Evan and Ty. Understand what motivates them so I can target a marketing plan accordingly."

She snorted. "Money. Market Share." Her eyes practically twinkled as she paused. "That makes them sound awful. They're really lovely people, they're just focused on success."

"You don't approve?" And why did her opinion matter? It would be easier if she didn't understand, if that could be another barrier between them. He needed all the barriers he could find to keep her on the wrong side of wanting him.

She shrugged. "It can be a lonely path."

He'd call it solitary. Last night had been fun, but he'd been happy to head home to his condo on the far side of the city and leave the noise behind. "To each their own."

She gave him a thoughtful look and nodded, but it was a distancing action. Like she'd measured him and found him wanting. As she should. He slid the materials she'd given him into his bag, double fisted his Americanos and escaped to the boardroom.

He littered the table with notes, big and small, and channeled his grumpiness into productivity. When she popped her head in the door, her long brown hair swinging around her face like a curtain, he was surprised that the morning had passed so quickly. "Is it lunch already?"

She winced. "Something's actually come up. Could we do it tomorrow?"

It was for the best. He'd make the excuse the next day, she could do the one after that. He nodded coolly and turned back to his work, tossing a muttered acknowledgement over his shoulder.

But as soon as she was gone, he regretted all that had been silently said in that moment, and sprinted after her. He stepped onto the open landing just in time to see her walk out the front door with another man, his arm wrapped around her waist.

— —

Finn was waiting in Beth's office when she got back from her lunch with Peter. It had been a nice distraction from the sex god working just down the hall. Everything about Peter was nice. He never made her screech.

Which is precisely why they were on date seven and still at the gentle making out stage. They'd done a little bit of that in the parking lot when he dropped her off, and it had been...nice. She'd been happy about that until she saw Finn sitting behind her desk. Then the fact that she could still feel the soft press of Peter's lips made her mad. Why couldn't she feel for him what she couldn't help but feel for this man? And how awful was she for wanting someone else when she was exploring a relationship with Peter?

Well, relationship was way over-stating things. They'd barely gotten to second base. And when he'd asked her if she was free for dinner on Friday night, she'd made up an excuse about work.

Great, now she was lying to a very nice man. Because of...him. "What are you doing in my chair?" She didn't need to layer any extra ice on her words. They were chilly enough on their own.

"It's more comfortable than the ones in the boardroom." Equally cold, his retort made her see red.

"I have some calls to make. You need to leave."

He stared at her, his dark eyes hard and unyielding. She stood her ground. He needed to get out of her office, now, before she did something she'd regret. As if he understood and didn't really care, he smirked and stood, coming around the desk. "Does lunch with your boyfriend always make you so bitchy?"

She gasped. "Excuse me?"

"I didn't realize you were seeing someone." His voice, cold and pointed, didn't match the odd expression on his face, but she was too incensed to parse the difference.

"I didn't realize it was any of your business."

He was close enough she could see a vein pulse on his temple as he clenched his jaw. "Didn't say it was."

A throbbing pain made itself known in the middle of her forehead. "Then why—"

"Forget it. I was out of line." He moved to brush past her and without thinking she reached out and grabbed his arm. He froze and looked down at that point of contact, then trailed his gaze up her arm and onto her face. It took him what felt like forever and by the time his eyes met hers she'd stopped breathing. "Something else you want to say, Beth?"

His voice had changed, warmer and rougher now, and her name hung between them. She swiped her tongue nervously across her top lip, painfully aware that he was staring at her. "He's not my boyfriend." Why was she telling Finn? And wasn't Peter her boyfriend? No, not really. "We've gone out a few times and he dropped in to take me out for lunch. It's not...serious."

"It looked serious." Finn looked at her mouth again, and she felt her cheeks burn up. Had he seen them kissing in the parking lot? She wouldn't feel guilty about that. You can't cheat on a fantasy. "When you were walking out. He had his arm around you."

Relief warred with confusion, but Beth wasn't up for thinking too hard about either point, not with Finn this close to her. Oh, so close. Had he shifted? Another few inches and they'd be pressed against one another. She needed to erect a wall between them before she did something stupid like pull him closer. Being rejected would make this whole exchange that much worse."Well, maybe there's still potential there. Anyway, not a subject we need to discuss further, right?"

She lifted her hand and took a wide step around him, focusing on the papers on her desk and then out the window. Anything but looking back at Finn. His response did not matter. Don't look.

She turned and looked. He was gone. She narrowed her eyes. It would be way too juvenile to pick up her stapler and wing it at the empty doorway. Also, inappropriate and possibly dangerous should anyone walk by.

Unless that someone was Finn. Beaning him in the head with her Swingline sounded like a fantastic idea. What a jerk, part of her subconscious said. The other part was replaying the hooded look he gave her as she licked her lips.

With a curse, she grabbed her handbag and headed out the door. No work was going to get done with Finn just down the hall. She needed some space to regroup. So much for the peace offerings of the morning.

As she blasted out the front doors, she almost ran over Liam McIntosh, the engineer overseeing the conversion of the manor house into a modern inn. He had his infant daughter, Ava, strapped to his chest in a sporty black baby carrier.

"Whoa there, Beth," he chuckled. "In a hurry?"

"Just heading into town for a meeting." A fib, but she could make it real by stopping at Bun In the Oven.

"Could you do me a favour?" He whipped a black backpack off his shoulder and tugged out a canvas pouch. "This is Max's communication envelope for school. It got stuck in the wrong bag this morning. Can you give it to

Evie? She's picking the boys up from school today, and we're stuck here waiting for the building inspector."

Beth smiled at Liam's use of the royal we. She reached out and stroked Ava's cheek. The five-month-old grinned right back, and Beth told her ovaries not to pay attention. They ignored her. "You're juggling a lot these days, eh? Sure, I can drop that off."

"Thanks a million!" Liam headed inside and Beth got in her car, thinking about Liam and his fiancée Evie and their newly blended family. A few years her junior, Liam hadn't blinked when Evie had a surprise pregnancy early in their relationship. How early no one was quite sure, but their unconventional start at love didn't fuel the Wardham gossip mill nearly as much as how perfectly suited to fatherhood Liam seemed to be.

Well, the old biddies were right—Liam was a DILF. The type of man Beth had always fantasized she'd end up with.

Finn's complete opposite.

Sure, they were both good looking. Dark hair, athletic builds. But that's where the similarities ended. No way in hell would Finn ever wear a baby carrier. He was probably allergic to children, a consideration that gnawed at Beth's gut.

When he wasn't being a complete asshole, when his voice got low and rough and his eyes softened, that was a Finn that she'd want to clone a hundred times over. When he worked around the clock to make sure that events went off without a hitch, quietly helping the smaller, understaffed wineries.

When he stared at her mouth. God. She shivered. Fantasy. Finn was a hypersexual person, a man's man who probably thought about sex every seven seconds and her mouth just happened to be the closest.

And that just lead to her thinking about what she could do with her mouth and his—

"Argh!" She yelled out loud and stomped on the gas, eager to get into town and away from her thoughts.

She parked in the middle of the block, halfway between Evie Calhoun's Pilates studio and Carrie Nixon's bakery/coffee shop. Wardham's two intersecting main streets were quiet in the early afternoon, and the early summer breeze off the lake fluttered the new 'Welcome to Wardham' banners.

When she started working at the winery, the village was known for its lovely beach and not much else. She thought she'd rent there for a while before settling in one of the larger towns nearby or moving on to another opportunity in a city. But when a new subdivision was built on the west end of town, she'd surprised herself by putting a down payment on a townhouse. This place was home now and she wouldn't have it any other way.

She'd even started to make some lovely friendships. Evan had introduced her to Karen Miller, who had temporarily moved to Toronto to study library science, but had trusted Beth to organize her wedding. Karen's now husband, Paul Reynolds, one of the OPP constables at the local detachment was another friendly face, and through them she'd gotten to know Evie and Carrie.

A little girl talk would be the perfect antidote to the ridiculous rage storm Finn conjured in her soul. First she'd pop in to see Evie, then head to Bun for yet another coffee.

But she didn't need to go as far as the studio out of the door stepped the blonde owner.

"Evie!" Beth waved the canvas folder in her direction. "Liam asked me to give this to you."

The other woman laughed. "He sent me a text. Can I buy you a coffee in thanks?"

"You read my mind. You've got time?"

Evie nodded. "Stella's teaching the next class."

Carrie's younger cousin had helped Evie at the studio across her pregnancy and when she couldn't teach classes immediately after Ava was born. "So she's still working for you?"

Evie winced. "Yeah. I can't really afford her for as many

classes as she's teaching, but she's awesome. I don't want to cut her back, because if she gets a full-time job, then I'm screwed."

Beth could commiserate. Managing casual staff herself, she knew someone leaving for greener pastures was a constant concern. "What kind of work is she looking for? I'm always looking for competent people to help at events." She dug a business card out of her purse. "If you don't mind sharing, tell her to send me a résumé."

"I don't mind at all, thank you!" Evie grinned. "I'm so glad you came into town."

Beth rolled her eyes. "I didn't have a choice. I needed to get away from work."

"Evan?" Evie sighed. "I know he can be...difficult."

Beth didn't know the whole backstory, but Evie and her boss had dated in high school. Beth was pretty sure her friend had been Evan's last girlfriend before he came out of the closet. They still seemed close. "He can, but he's away this week."

Evie pulled open the door to Bun. Carrie was refilling the muffin trays and Feist was playing out of the overhead speakers. For once, the place was empty.

"Carrie, this woman needs some cheering up—make her a latte!"

Beth groaned. "Actually, I've had enough coffee for one day. I'll take a green tea instead."

Evie twirled her fingers indicating Carrie should make two, which she did. As she slid them across the counter, she narrowed her eyes at Beth. "Did you end up drinking both coffees you bought this morning?"

She made a face. "No. It's a long story."

"We've got time," Evie said with an evil grin.

Beth couldn't help but laugh and then she gave them a brief rundown. The more confusing parts of Finn's behaviour she kept to herself.

Evie spoke first. "Finn Howard? I met him at the Networking Essex County luncheon last month. He seemed nice."

"He is nice." Carrie grinned. "To everyone except Beth. There's something about her that drives him mental."

"I bet it's your boobs." Evie brazenly gave her a once-over, and Beth crossed her arms over her chest, eliciting laughs from her friends. "Seriously, I've got cleavage envy. You know what's a total lie? That nursing makes your boobs bigger."

Carrie rolled her eyes. "Yeah, for the first few weeks when that's the last thing that you want. After that…" She blew a raspberry and gestured downwards with her hands.

Beth had enough friends with kids that this wasn't new information. That she didn't have firsthand experience…her ovaries rata-tat-tatted in her lower belly. She cleared her throat, refocusing herself and her friends. "My boobs don't drive him mental." *Although I'm starting to wonder if the man has a mouth fetish.* "It's just me. We're like oil and water. He hates all of my ideas. It's like he goes out of his way to be contrary."

Evie made a silent oh with her mouth and nodded sagely. "He's pulling your pig-tails."

So much for wisdom. "No. Finn hates me."

"It's a fine line between love and hate," Evie mused.

Beth rolled her eyes. "Oh, come on! You and Liam are like the perfect couple. I bet you never fight."

"Fight? No, that's not our style. I'm more of the cold-shoulder type. We snipe sometimes, though." She pointed across the counter at her redheaded friend. "But Carrie and Ian? They go at it like cats and dogs."

"You're missing out." Carrie laughed. "Make up sex is where it's at."

Beth had seen Ian pissed off one minute and hauling Carrie in for an X-rated kiss the next. She believed it. The Nixons had the type of passion country music songs were written about.

She'd take either kind of love, but she definitely wanted love. Not pigtail pulling from a man who couldn't see the harm in winding up old and alone. Who might want to stare at her mouth, and her legs when he thought she wasn't looking, but couldn't find three nice sentences to string together.

That's why she'd ditched lunch and gone with Peter instead. She needed to give nice another try. Nice would satisfy the ache in her ovaries, even if her heart would need some convincing to come around.

CHAPTER THREE

Finn watched Beth flip through the portfolio he'd slid across her desk five minutes earlier. She'd scratched a few notes here and there on Post-its but gave no hint as to her overall reaction.

It had been two weeks since their tense standoff in her office and they'd both retreated to their proverbial corners. Exchanges had been brief and professional, giving him lots of time to get the job done. Now that he'd laid out a blueprint for promotion and marketing, his day-to-day involvement at the winery could come to an end.

Disappointment wasn't his usual reaction to wrapping up a successful project. He watched—weak-ass way of saying he stared—as Beth absentmindedly twirled a long strand of dark hair around her finger. Her brows pulled together and she bit her lip, and he wanted to reach out and tug the soft, plump skin from between her teeth. Maybe replace it with his thumb. Press her mouth open and tease the pink point of her tongue. Call her a good girl and watch fire light up her eyes—

"Tell me about the event calendar."

His dirty thoughts stuttered to a halt. He cleared his throat and tried to focus. Who cared about marketing notes when his every fantasy sat across the desk and twirled a pen? "I've added the WECGA events in green. Those booth fees have been paid for, so it would be a minimal expense to send staff for part of the weekend. The bigger wineries do this, and it's time Go West joined their ranks."

"This is good, but it's too much." She blinked twice and

rubbed the back of her hand across her forehead. He could see the conflict battling in her mind. Visibility. He'd heard her concerns and put together a plan that satisfied that goal and also meshed with Evan and Ty's vision for their company. "We have a wedding with site tours next weekend. There's no way we can handle both the Windsor Wine and Cheese show and this new event in Toronto as well."

His gaze flicked to the paper in her hand, then back to her face. "Which one do you want me to do?"

She shook her head. "That's not your role. And whatever outrageous fee you're charging Evan is way above the fifteen an hour I pay my part-timers."

He leaned forward, bracing his arms against her desk. "I'll eat the time as a goodwill gesture."

"I didn't think you believed in goodwill." Her eyes flashed with hungry fight. She was pissed because it would be hard, not because it was wrong.

He forced calm into his response. "I thought we'd moved past the barbed statements, Beth."

"Force of habit, I apologize." But instead of the words floating out with the breezy conviction she probably intended, her voice warbled with honest regret and he wanted to kiss the fight right out of her. It wasn't her way— it was his. He made her like this and she hated it. "But you still don't need to do me any favours."

"Would it make you feel better if I told you I have an ulterior motive?" He pushed away from her desk and shoved his hands in his pockets, sweeping his suit jacket out of the way.

"And what would that be?"

Could he trust her? He knew her first reaction wouldn't be good. But he could push past that. Break through the crap between them and finally put it all on the table.

"I'm starting my own business. A consulting firm."

— —

"A consulting firm." She repeated the words slowly, rolling them over in her mouth. She didn't like the way they tasted. Like duplicity, an unexpected sourness. "So this—" she tossed the portfolio on the desk "—was what, a test project? An example of your work to show potential clients?" She barely held back a sneer. "I'm sure Evan will provide you with a positive reference."

He dipped his head, his gaze hooded but still pinned on her. "And you wouldn't?"

"I can't be objective. I'd refer all calls to Evan, though. I wouldn't say anything negative."

"But you think negatively of me?" He was a hard man, made of steel, but something in his words grabbed her attention. Like her opinion mattered.

She licked her lips. Did he bump into the thermometer on his way in? It was suddenly a million degrees in her office. "Our tendency toward conflict—"

"Has nothing to do with work." Rough, vibrating honesty.

Liquid panic flooded her body. She couldn't handle a truthful exploration of the impossible messiness between them. She'd built a mansion in Denialville and never planned to move out. "I don't think negatively of you." Her words flowed fast, spurred by fear and desperate self-preservation. "We're very different, that's all."

"So this tension simmering between us—you chalk that up to personality conflict?" He shrugged out of his jacket and folded it over the back of a chair. He moved with fluid grace, suddenly reminding her of a panther, right down to the dark shiny hair and predator eyes.

"Yes," she whispered.

He stalked around her desk and held out his hand. How was he not shaking? She was a leaf in the wind, and his large hand with those beautiful long fingers held steady in her swimming vision. "Stand up."

She shook her head, unable to respond.

"Beth." Oh god, her name on his tongue was magic, and

she watched herself reach out and slide her fingers against his. "We just need to get this out of our systems."

She shook her head, even as he tugged her out of her chair and shifted her so she was sitting on the edge of her desk. "You've gone mad."

"Absolutely." He nodded and reached out to brush her hair behind her ear. His fingers lingered there, tracing the curving cartilage to the soft lobe. "You always wear the most distracting earrings. I like these, but the sparkly green ones on Thursday were probably my favourite."

Flip. Her internal organs rioted, not giving two figs if her head thought this was a terrible idea. She tilted her head, showing him the long stretch of her neck. Practically begging him to touch her there, and he obliged, trailing his fingers down to her collarbone and then back up again, lifting her chin. She swallowed. "You notice my earrings."

"I notice everything about you, Beth. At first it was your legs and your smile. Then your laugh. I've wanted to kiss you since the day I met you."

She wanted to ask why he hadn't, but as quickly as the question slipped into her head, the answer followed. Because he'd realized they wouldn't be good together. Those personality differences did matter, and just like that, all those heady endorphins lost their magical effect.

But he was right in front of her, and from the look in his eyes he knew she was about to run—and he wasn't going to let her.

"There's a reason we went in the direction we did, Finn." She straightened her spine. "Attraction is just one factor, and all others indicate this is a terrible idea."

"It's the most important factor, though. And this isn't just attraction." He lowered his voice to a near whisper, his words licking against her skin. "It's chemistry. I've tried to fight it, for all the reasons I'm sure you'd love to hide behind. But the truth is, I want to kiss you more than I've ever wanted to kiss anyone and that's not going away."

"We don't always get what we want." I'm not going to

get gorgeous dark haired, grey-eyed toddlers. I'm going to end up with a broken heart and a Finn-shaped voodoo doll. Probably a half-dozen cats and a teacup collection. "You've probably built this up in your head. Not used to being denied and all that."

"Are you denying me?" His face was close enough she couldn't focus on both his eyes and his mouth at the same time, but she saw the curve of his lips and knew she was done like dinner.

She slowly shook her head, not breaking eye contact. She wanted to stare into those dark grey pools forever, but then his nose brushed hers and everything went fuzzy in the split second before his lips pressed against hers, firm and warm, and she was gone.

This was no beginner's touch. It might be the first and last time they gave in to the fire between them, and neither would waste the opportunity. His lips quickly parted, his teeth nipping at her lower lip and when she gasped, his tongue darted out to sooth the injured flesh. That erotic touch drew her own response and the first taste of Finn's mouth only sharpened her hunger for him. She brought her hands to cup his face, still newly shaved, and the silky smooth skin over clenched muscle and sharp jaw made her cry out at the perfection of it all.

She was kissing Finn Howard and it was everything she thought it would be and more. As if he could sense that she was falling apart, he braced his arms behind her, tangling one hand in her hair and planting the other on her desk, canted at an angle behind her hip.

He had her. And she wanted more. She shifted her hips right to the edge of the desk, her pelvis acting with a mind of its own, looking for…ahhhh. Finn groaned before she realized she'd made contact with his erection, but a split second later the awareness settled in and she needed that against her core. She wrapped one leg around his hip, vaguely aware of his hand moving, sliding up her bare thigh and curling around the outside to behind her knee. And then he was holding her open and rocking against her, his tongue fucking into her mouth, mimicking what she desperately needed at her very centre.

Somewhere in the distance a phone rang, and she realized she was about to have sex on her desk in the middle of the day. Her office door was unlocked. With a gasp, she wrenched her mouth free and shoved Finn away.

He spun on the spot and smacked his hand against the floor-to-ceiling window behind her desk. In the quiet of her office, they took matching ragged breaths. In. Out.

Holy fuck. The ache between her legs and the heaviness of her breasts reminded her it wasn't quite that—but it had certainly been more than a kiss. She slid off her desk and yanked her skirt back into position. When Finn turned around, she was still standing there, her fingers pressed against her mouth.

He stared at her hand for a minute. "I'm not going to apologize for what just happened."

She lifted her chin. "I'm not asking you to."

"But that didn't work exactly as I expected it to." He frowned, and she realized for the first time that he must be biting his inner cheek when he did that. She didn't know what to make of that.

"I could say the same thing." A non-response, but she wasn't sure where he was going. He was clearly bothered by what they'd just done. Well, too bad. That bell couldn't be un-rung. It would be awkward for a while, but they hadn't been fooling anyone with their previous awkwardness either.

"There's just one solution." He took a deep sigh and strode around her desk, pausing just long enough to swing his jacket back on. "We're going to need to do that again. With the door locked next time."

Beth gaped as he strode out of her office without giving her a chance to respond. Oh, hell no. They definitely weren't doing that again.

CHAPTER FOUR

THEY hadn't done it again. Kissing or anything else. He'd thought about it, a lot, but when he returned to her office later that day Evan was with her. The older West brother had just finished reassuring Beth that he would cover the Toronto event and any other high profile but far afield events on the calendar.

Finn felt like punching something. So much for his chance to be the white knight. So he'd slinked off. The next day he'd called her and left a message. The day after that, he sent an email. She took a full twenty-four hours to respond, and when she did it was business only.

A slow burning fuse started in his gut. He'd give her some time, but he wasn't waiting forever. Not when he'd had a taste of just how responsive Beth Stewart was in his arms.

A kiss. That was all it should have been.

Blazing hell. He'd been a minute away from sinking into her hot, wet heat. The vivid memory of her grinding against him was seared onto his frontal lobe.

He'd be back in Wardham for a follow up meeting in another week, but he couldn't wait that long to see her. And if their next meeting was on her territory, she'd probably ensure one of the West brothers was there as a guardian of sorts.

A better man would take her hastily constructed barriers as a clear sign of disinterest. Instead, Finn's desire to have Beth flipped into overdrive.

And if she were keen, you wouldn't be, because you're a

bastard. He couldn't deny it. He'd always been a fan of pursuit. Seduce, conquer, move on.

He wouldn't move on right away, of course. She'd be wary of him, and that would keep him hooked. They'd date. He liked dating. It made sense to him. Orderly and mutually satisfying, with clear boundaries and multiple exit opportunities.

But this...disgruntlement he felt, this didn't make sense. He shoved back from his breakfast bar and stalked to the sink. He dumped what remained of his cereal in the garbage under the counter and washed the bowl. This was the first Saturday in a month he didn't have any work to do. He should write articles for his website or go to the market and glad-hand there. Always be networking. The mantra rolled through his head. But he didn't feel like it. He felt like finding a certain brunette bombshell and dragging her into the nearest dark corner.

He recognized the itchy heat crawling up his back. He'd felt the same way about working in sports broadcasting when he was in college. He'd wanted that television internship in a painful way, been desperate for it...and when he lost out, and ended up at a radio station instead, he'd been gutted. Almost hadn't made the most of that opportunity.

But he'd talked sense into himself then, and he would here.

Wanting Beth wasn't going to take over his life.

He needed a solid dose of reality so he threw on some running clothes. He'd head over to one of his sisters' houses and let the chaos refocus his mind on what really mattered.

— —

Beth hovered her thumb over the green button on her screen. She'd assumed Peter had moved on when she turned down his next few invitations, but this morning's voice mail invitation to join him in the city for a group picnic and ultimate frisbee game was too tempting to pass up.

Putting herself back on the market would be a good first step to getting over Finn's kiss.

To getting over Finn.

She rubbed her chest, as if she could reach the sad ache from the outside and erase it with her touch. She knew it didn't work like that.

She was in charge of her own happiness. She needed to replace that sadness with something better. Healthier. Something good and fun like a picnic. She pressed call and committed herself to another kick at the can.

— —

"Unca Finn, you can be the boy Barbie. Here you go." Tasha pressed a naked Ken doll into his hand.

Finn looked down at the poor dickless bastard. "Boy Barbie needs some pants, Tasha."

"No." The four-year-old shook her head solemnly. "He's potty training. Just like Jake."

Her younger brother cruised by at that moment, his naked bottom making more sense now, and Finn surreptitiously glanced around for puddles.

From behind him, Sienna laughed and he twisted to give his middle sister a stern look. It didn't work. "Jeez, Finn, scared of a little pee?"

Yes, and the diapers and college tuition that come with it. "To each their own."

"Has anyone ever argued you on that point?"

He shrugged and walked Ken over to the outdoor grill behind Barbie's mansion. Fire and naked plastic crotch seemed like a good combination. "Who wants steak?"

His little sister ruffled his hair as she swept past him. "Do you want to stay for dinner? We could do steaks for real. Janine's bringing her kids over for a movie night."

"I'll come back for the movie, but I've got some work to do this afternoon." He'd made his bed. To each their own, and his own was being a workaholic. At least he could take some solace in the fact he was good at it.

— —

"This was a great way to spend a Saturday afternoon." Beth grinned at Peter over the cooler she was packing up.

He returned the smile and nodded at the field. "Do you want to learn how to play?"

She shook her head. "I'm good with being a cheerleader."

His gaze raked down to her bare legs and back up again and she blushed. "Works for me, too."

"Pete—"

He held up his hand. "I know. Nothing wrong with a little flirting, though. It's good practice."

"Flirting leads to kissing."

"How presumptuous, Ms. Stewart." He waggled his eyebrows.

She waved her hands in defeat and laughed. "You win, flirting is allowed." She glanced around the picnic area. "It looks like someone stole the garbage can. I think I have some garbage bags in my trunk. I'll be right back."

Her car was in the parking lot on the far side of the gazebo and swimming pools and it took her a few minutes to walk across the park. On the way, she reflected on the new friendship she'd settled into with Peter. Not necessarily lasting or close, but comfortable. Maybe nice had its uses after all.

She remotely popped the trunk of her car, grabbed a garbage bag and a spare bottle of water, and turned to head back, only to stumble over her footsteps as Finn jogged across her path. He slowed to a stop and lifted his hand in greeting, but didn't say anything.

Time slowed as excitement from the unexpected encounter slammed into panic. They'd kissed and she'd dodged his calls. Like a coward. What could she say to him?

"Hi," she offered lamely.

He looked far too delicious for someone in the midst of exercising. A dark grey technical t-shirt stretched across his shoulders and stuck to his long, flat stomach. Black shorts hinted at strong thighs and led to sculpted calves covered evenly in dark hair. Blood pounded in her ears as she took in the masculine totality of him. She didn't hear him say her name until he repeated it and reached out to touch her shoulder.

"What are you doing here?" His expression shifted, like a mask sliding into place, and he offered an easy grin that covered a lot of unspoken questions. "You're far from home."

"Picnic with friends." It wasn't a lie. Peter's friends were nice, and she'd probably see them again at some point. Since her luck was exactly that awful, though, Peter took that moment to come strolling down the path with the cooler. They'd parked next to each other. There was no way Finn wouldn't see him. Her heart slammed against her chest wall and she wiped her hands on her shorts. "You remember Peter?" She gestured toward the other man. "His friends."

Finn stiffened and glanced over his shoulder, taking his time turning away and then sliding back. And when he did, the easy smile was gone and his eyes glittered with cold injury. The hurt there took her breath away but then he blinked and it was gone, leaving just cool acceptance in its place. "The boyfriend."

She opened her mouth to—confirm? Deny? She couldn't find either set of words, and then Peter was abreast of them.

He nodded to the cooler. "We're wrapping up quickly—thought I'd stash this away." He glanced between Beth and Finn and set the cooler down, extending a hand to Finn. "Hey, I'm Peter. A friend of Beth's."

"Finn." No explanation, but he accepted the greeting.

"We work together," Beth offered, desperately wanting the awkwardness to be over. Wishing she'd stayed at home and done laundry or painted her toenails instead of coming to Windsor.

Finn slid a look at her reminding her that they'd leapt over the colleagues line a week earlier and she owed him a conversation at the very least. The possession and demand in his eyes made her want to scream even as the memory of their kiss swept warmth through her core. As if he could tell, he shifted half a step toward her. Their arms brushed and that her first reaction was to slide her fingers into his was for sure a sign she'd gotten too much sun.

Finn Howard didn't hold hands. He devoured women, probably with decadent and impressive talent, then moved on. His possessive play here was only because he hadn't yet possessed. She didn't need to comfort him. He didn't have a heart. Couldn't be hurt, not really. Wounded pride wasn't her problem.

"Nice to meet you." Peter stowed away the cooler, then turned back to Beth, doing a bang up job of ignoring the simmering tension he'd stumbled across. She flashed him a small smile. "I'm going to give Stacey a ride home. If I don't see you before you head out…today was fun."

She murmured a quiet agreement and he disappeared. Nice guy. Damn. She took her time rolling her gaze back to Finn's face. When she got there she was shocked to find something that looked a lot like desire.

"Were you expecting me to be upset about your little lie?" he asked thickly, closing the space between them. He smelled like sports wash with a faint salty edge, and she wanted to lick him up.

"I didn't lie," she whispered. "You assumed."

"He's not your boyfriend."

She shook her head.

"So I don't need to feel guilty for wanting to kiss you again." He cupped her cheeks in both of his hands and dusted a light kiss across her lips. Double damn. He should feel guilty, but not for leading her astray. For being irresistible despite having zero future potential. Finn would never be her boyfriend, either, so he shouldn't taste so perfect. It was rude.

"This is a terrible idea." Even as she said it, she was leaning into him for another PG-13 caress.

"I agree. We're in the middle of a public park. I can't kiss you the way you want to be kissed until we're in private."

Yes. "No. Finn, we can't do this."

— —

He immediately took a step back. Beth was conflicted on that boundary, but no meant no. It didn't mean walk away with his tail between his legs, though. "I'd like a chance to convince you we can."

She tilted her head to the side in wary consideration. "Now?"

He glanced down at his running gear. It would have to do. She was wearing shorts that showed enough of her shapely calves and lush thighs that he'd been actively talking his dick out of a chubby since he first saw her, and a navy blue t-shirt that snugged around her curves in all the right ways. She looked better than him, by a long shot, but they weren't so mismatched they couldn't grab a cup of coffee or something. "I'm pretty sure I heard your friend say he was heading out soon. Now might be the perfect time. We could go to a coffee shop, or you could come back to my place."

She laughed, an honest trill that he wanted to feel vibrating through her skin. "I'm not going to your place." If I do, we'll do a lot more than kissing, her eyes warned. Ha. Warned. That felt like a promise, one he wanted to hold her to.

"Coffee, then." He liked the idea of sitting down with her and talking about something other than work. Indecision creased her brow and he leaned forward, close enough for his words to be intimate but not crossing that line she'd drawn. "What's the worst that could happen?"

It turned out the worst was forty-five minutes of watching Beth lick foamed milk from the top of her latte while she asked him questions about his family. Pure torture on many levels. He reached across the table and snagged her hand. "Listing all my nieces and nephews and their various after school activities is not what I was thinking about when I suggested we get a drink."

Her eyes danced with laughter but her pink cheeks and a flutter at the base of her neck reminded him he made her nervous. Tread lightly. "I'm jealous. I don't have a big family."

"No?" What the hell, Finn? You shouldn't care about her family. Maybe not, but she did.

"I'm an only child to two only children. I have pseudo cousins—my dad's best friend's kids—but they live in Vancouver."

"You're from the west coast?"

She nodded. Every time she did that her dark brown ponytail bounced over her shoulder in one glorious curl, practically begging him to wrap it around his hand and tug. Toward him for a kiss. Back so he could kiss down her neck. Down…his brain stuttered on that particular fantasy and he realized she was talking. Answering your question. "And after three years in Calgary, I put everything I owned in my Ford Escape and came east. I was headed for Halifax, but I wanted to visit Pelee Island."

Finn smirked. "I've lived here my entire life and I've never been."

She rolled her eyes. "Why am I not surprised? It's the southern most tip of Canada—you have to go!"

"I've heard it's quaint."

"You say that like it's a bad thing." She smiled. "You can rent bicycles and ride around the island."

"That sounds awful."

"Hmmm." She turned the appraising noise into a sensual challenge. "You're an interesting guy."

That wasn't at all what he expected her to say, and he burst out laughing. When he wasn't pissing her off, Beth found him interesting. Instead of sending fear straight to his heart, that made him want to share more. Make her eyes twinkle. She won't find your mercurial ways interesting for long. Maybe that would be okay. Maybe they could go into this with eyes wide open. "Maybe I need to tell you all the other things I don't appreciate in this world."

Her lips curled into a soft smile. "Small children, slow drivers and jogging pants as everyday wear?"

"Three for three. But none of those make you hum like you did before." He leaned forward and traced his index finger from her delicate wrist up the swell of her forearm. Her skin was soft and silky, her curves endless and addictive.

"I hear you on the Sunday drivers, and I appreciate a tailored suit. But kids are a deal breaker for me." She pressed her hand on top of his, stilling his exploration of her skin. "I'm at an age where dating has become…purposeful."

He opened his mouth, but no response came out. What could he say? Who said anything about dating? Except he'd thought about it, just not with the same focus she had. Beth wasn't saying anything he hadn't told himself many times over. She wasn't that type of woman. And the thought of someone using her for a quick roll in the hay made him see red. What a joke. The only asshole considering that was sitting right there. Being shot down before he'd even suggested it.

"It's not that I don't like kissing you—" She cut herself off abruptly and turned pink. That flush ran a live wire to his groin because he was a total bastard. But it also sparked something new and unfamiliar in his chest. A protective instinct he thought he'd only ever feel for his sisters. Maybe that's what fate intended for them…their paths weren't meant to ever intersect, but run parallel.

Their relationship had changed so much in a few short weeks. Even as she let him down, he wanted to hang on to the delicate friendship they might be able salvage from the wreckage of their almost fling.

"Maybe the chemistry between us means something else," he offered, his voice gruff and foreign to his own ears.

He reached across the table and pulled her hand back to his, tangling their fingers together. "Like we should be…friends."

She glanced at their hands twisted together, then back up at his face. Doubt radiated off her. "Friends?"

"What about that do you find so unbelievable? I have friends." None that he wanted to strip naked and lick from head to toe, but there was a first time for everything. "You were telling me about what kept you here."

She wrinkled her brow and cleared her throat. "Finn, this is—"

"This is worth a try." He offered his most winning smile. "Come on. Did you meet Evan on the island?"

She pressed the tip of her tongue to her upper lip for a moment, then sighed and smiled. Gotcha. "Nothing that coincidental. I went for a tour of the winery on the island, and was surprised to learn just how many different wineries there were in region. It seemed like a good match for my work experience and college diploma."

"Hospitality and Tourism?" Her eyes widened in surprise. "Someone told me." Because he'd asked.

"Ah. Yes. And there was a flyer for a job fair on the bulletin board. The rest, as they say, is history." She took a sip of coffee before segueing the conversation back to Finn. She grilled him on how he'd moved from broadcasting to marketing and his plans for a consulting firm.

Before he knew it, another hour had passed and their coffees were long gone. Beth yawned, and immediately apologized. "I should get going."

The look on her face told him she felt the same reluctance to leave he did, like the stars aligning and allowing them to have a nice conversation might never happen again. No. He was done antagonizing her. Done goading her just to feel the heat of her gaze tearing into his skin. Their future didn't lie in passion and he needed to let that go.

The consolation prize of her friendship would have to be good enough.

CHAPTER FIVE

"What's going on with you and Finn?"

Beth looked up from the schedule she was revising with a start. Evan West loomed large in her doorway, a frown on his face. Handsome in a totally different way than his brother, although they shared the same wavy hair—and probably the same expensive salon stylist—and piercing blue eyes. But Evan was dark and intense to Ty's laid-back personality, and it started with the heavier-than-usual furrow between his eyebrows.

"Nothing…" She pursed her lips and put down her pen. "Why?"

"He was nice to you at the meeting this morning." Evan prowled into her office and looked over her shoulder. "Is that next week's schedule?"

"Yes. Don't change the subject. If you're going to meddle, do it right."

"I'm multi-tasking." He circled his finger around a penciled in name. "You've hired little Stella Nixon?"

"She's twenty-three."

"Shit, I'm old."

She burst out laughing. "Sure are. Can we get back to why you're interrupting me?"

"I liked Finn better when he was busting your chops." Evan worked his jaw back and forth, and understanding dawned.

Beth pushed back from her desk and stood, staring her boss and friend in the eye. "Are you here to warn me about Finn's philandering ways?"

"You're not his usual type. I don't want you to get hurt."

She rolled her eyes and patted Evan on the chest, turning him at the same time and pointing him toward the door. "Finn and I are not involved." *Unless you count my fantasies late at night. Then we're very busy doing things that might be illegal in some parts of the world.* "We've decided to be friends. It's much less exhausting than enemies."

Evan took a few steps, retreating out of slapping range, then shook his head. "He's never looked at you like an enemy, Beth."

She desperately wanted to hear more about how Finn used to look at her—and ask if he still did when she wasn't looking—but no one could know how much she didn't want to be Finn's friend. Not Evan, not her friends at Bun, and definitely not Finn. Because what she wanted and what Finn was offering—no, had offered, and now retracted—were diametrically opposed ideas. A relationship, complicated and messy and loaded with potential for the future. Or an...arrangement. Carefully delineated by smooth words at the outset meant to take the sting out of a casual goodbye at end.

She wasn't interested.

An affair. That was his way, and she wouldn't be the first. Or the last. The thought of Finn rolling around in the sheets with women he didn't care about made her want to vomit. And she had absolutely no right to that reaction, but it would be a billion times worse if they slept together. She'd want to rain hellfire down on him if he blithely moved on from her and since she wasn't a Valkyrie but just an ordinary Director of Operations and Guest Services at a winery, and the worst she could actually do was refuse to sell him a bottle of wine, well...she didn't really want to wander down that path of impotent rage.

So she needed to get him out of her system before these enquiries started to trump their day-to-day work.

"We're just friends." She said it once, then repeated it,

following Evan to the door which she closed once he was safely on the other side. But being alone wasn't better, because in the silence Evan's words bounced effortlessly off the walls and into her soul. *He's never looked at you like an enemy.*

— —

That thought stuck with her when she headed down to the tasting room to check on Stella's training session with Gavin Beadie, one of their bartenders. He had a blind taste test set up and Stella was carefully comparing each sip to her notes before tentatively naming the wine. Gavin was good. Beth had seen him do this training before and after a few sessions all of their casual staff could talk with some authority about the product lines.

Gavin was a part-time student, studying literature at the university in Windsor, and had shown no interest in taking on a larger role in the organization despite repeated offers. Beth would just be happy to have him behind her bar as long as he was willing. And Gavin joked that he had two younger brothers who could be trained as bartenders if she needed them, because it was in their blood—his twin sister Mari was also a bartender, at the pub in town, and had helped Beth out with a few early events before referring Gavin to her for the regular gig.

It surprised Beth that Mari hadn't been the one to send Stella her way, as the two young women were close. Maybe it was her unsettled state of mind, but something made her more curious than usual about Stella, what made her tick, and how the shy young woman had ended up sending her a bold and entertaining cover letter and résumé a few hours after Beth had given Evie her card. So when Gavin excused himself to bring up more wine from the basement, Beth settled in next to her new employee and poured herself a glass of wine. It was five o'clock somewhere. Being the boss had to have some perks.

39

She leaned against the bar and smiled at Stella. "It sounds like you're catching on quickly."

The younger woman blushed. "I hope so."

"Are you a wine drinker?"

Stella shrugged. "With a holiday meal. Once in a blue moon with girlfriends."

"I listened for a bit. You've picked up the lingo quickly."

"It's not that different from maple syrup grades." Stella bit her lip. "I mean, of course it's not the same thing, but—"

"It's okay." Beth reached out and pressed a reassuring hand on Stella's shoulder. "Maple syrup?"

"It's one of the crops on our farm. We have two sugar bushes on our property and there are two more on my uncles' farms not far from us."

"What else do you farm?"

"Soybeans, corn, alfalfa. Cash crops. But it's just me and my dad, so the last few years, most of our profits have been paid out in wages. The sugar bush is the only part that we do entirely ourselves."

Beth wasn't a farm girl herself, but she'd lived in Wardham long enough to know it was a tough life and getting harder every year. "That's why you're working with Evie and at the police station?"

Thoughts more complicated than Beth could guess at clouded across Stella's face. "That's part of it." She reached for her glass of wine and when she turned back, her eyes were clear and curious. "How did you end up with your career?"

Beth shook her head and smiled. "You know, I was just telling a friend about it on the weekend. Luck and happenstance get most of the credit. And being willing to do a lot of grunt work. The first year that I was the Promotions Coordinator here, I really did a lot of envelope stuffing, box unpacking, and floor and window washing. And I spent a lot of time behind this bar." She patted her hand on the polished wood surface. "Over time, I did more and was rewarded with greater responsibility." She laughed. "Some days that doesn't feel like much of a reward, but overall it's been wonderful. Is that what you're looking for, a career?"

Stella widened her eyes for a second, as if it was a trick question. Beth pushed as much reassurance into her own expression as she could muster, and it must have done the trick. "Right now, I'm just looking for work. Happy to do whatever will get me off the farm. Which is probably the height of irony, because in the long term I'd love to take it over from my dad. But I'm too old to live at home and he's too young to retire to a house in town."

"It's just the two of you?" That would be a claustrophobic life for a woman in her twenties.

"My sister lives in Toronto. My mom…she visits. My parents have a weird and complicated relationship."

Beth gasped. "You're Marigold Nixon's daughter!"

Stella rolled her eyes. "Her real name is Meredith, but yes."

"She's a wonderful artist." Beth watched Stella shift uncomfortably in her chair. "You hear that a lot."

"It's true. But she hasn't been an involved parent. It's okay, I've never known anything different."

But it wasn't okay. Beth's parents both worked, and her mother had travelled a fair bit when she was younger, doing guest lectures at universities across North America. Yet when she came home, she was home, and Beth never doubted her mother missed her while away. Something told her Stella hadn't received that kind of reassurance as a child and still wanted it as an adult. She recognized that yearning. Felt it herself for her father's affection. He'd been home more than her mother but not nearly as present or engaged.

But this wasn't the time or place and she was assuming a lot. Maybe another time, another shared bottle of wine.

"Well, I'm glad you enjoy working here. That's why I came down, actually, to confirm you're doing the Patterson wedding this weekend. I've posted both the revised schedule for next week and the open one for the next two weeks. Let me know if you have any questions." She'd moved all the employees to a web-based scheduling software suite. It took a bit more training up front but saved a lot of time over the long haul.

Gavin returned as she was talking and she left them to finish up before the anticipated arrival of a tour group.

Back in her office, Beth glanced at her notes from the morning's meeting. She reached for her favourite pink highlighter just as her phone rang. A quick glance at the call display made her heart skip a beat. Just friends.

"Beth Stewart." Smooth and sexy. At least she hoped.

"Finn Howard." He chuckled as he mimicked her.

"I was just looking at what we talked about this morning."

"Me too."

She tapped her notepad. "You gave us notes on amping up the Christmas party and speed dating around Valentine's Day. You didn't have any notes about the Winter Tea." He hesitated long enough to give her a big clue. "You don't like it."

"I don't see what it does for your brand."

"It's a hug hit with our loyal customers! We've sold out each of the last three years."

"Do it for them, but it's not something to promote to new people. It muddies the water."

"It shows we're a winery for everyone."

"You can't be."

"Of course we can." She heard the strident tone slip into her voice before she could rein it back. This is when we fight. The realization caught like a lump in her throat and unexpected sadness washed over Beth. How tenuous that claim of friendship proved to be.

But instead of snapping, Finn laughed. Warm and low, like they were sharing a joke. "Why won't you just let me tell you what to do?"

Her own laugh was watery and weak, terribly unsure of itself. "That sounds dangerous." In more ways than one. She took a deep breath. "I'm scared to narrow our focus to the younger demographic."

"Ah. Now we're getting somewhere." He made a thinking noise, somewhere between a hum and a growl, and she had to press her legs together. Finn at work…that turned her on in a big way. Even when he was pissing her off, and today he'd managed not to do that. "If I can show you numbers that prove there's money to be made in targeting the right audience, will you give me more room to play with your event calendar?"

She smiled, kicked off her shoes and swayed her office chair from side to side. "What kind of numbers?"

"I'll double your Facebook fan numbers by the end of the month, and the new likes will be in the target demographic."

She snorted. "Easily done with an ad buy."

He tsked in her ear and her nipples stood up and took notice. Down girls, he's off-limits. "No ad buy."

"Then how—"

He cut her off with that hum-growl noise again. "That's for me to know and for you to be suitably impressed by at the end of the month."

He had a deal, but she didn't need to seem eager. She bit her lip to contain her glee at negotiating her way through a business conversation without wanting to shake Finn. She counted down from ten before assuming her smooth, sexy voice. "I look forward to that meeting."

"We can discuss it further on Saturday."

She shot straight up in her chair, limbs akimbo and sexy voice abandoned. "What?" she screeched, then slammed her palm to her forehead as he chuckled in her ear.

"We'll both be at the Windsor Wine and Food Show."

Crap. Their friendship worked best in limited quantities. She cleared her throat and concentrated on sounding cool again. "I may find a replacement for my shift."

"No you won't." He lowered his voice. "You want to see me as much as I want to see you."

"Is that a fact?" But they both knew it was.

— —

Finn pulled up to the Willistead Manor service entrance where his intern, Kent, waited with a handcart. They unloaded the boxes of WECGA postcards and promotional corkscrews from his trunk. Many of their member wineries would have individual displays given the proximity to home but he'd brought enough swag just in case any of them ran out.

The historic mansion was the perfect venue for this event. He allowed himself a moment of self-congratulation at the choice before moving his car to the back of the parking lot and heading inside.

In addition to vintners, the show had displays from catering companies, high-end food shops, artisanal cheese makers and a couple of organic food co-ops and community share farms. Finn sat on the steering committee and he'd supported the chair's decision to ruthlessly slim down the event to fit it into the new space.

Inside, he automatically scanned the room for Beth.

Want throbbed in his abdomen. Beth. The one desire he hadn't managed to mould to his satisfaction. Their goals didn't align and she had proved more than once to be his match for sticking to her guns.

He found her halfway between her booth and the end of the aisle. He stopped at the far end of the room and just watched as she glad-handed her way up the row. She wore pants today, slim black dress trousers that cupped her ass and made her legs look a mile long. At the end of those delicious legs were black heels that made his mind blank. She was probably 5'6" without them, but he realized he'd never seen her in flats. Even at the park she'd worn casual shoes with a wedge lift. He was struck by a sudden desire to see her totally unwrapped, wearing nothing but his dress shirt. A small, curvy, perfect package. Because while her heels were sexy, he realized that wasn't why she wore them.

They were a power tactic, to bring her eye to eye with the men around her.

Irrationally, he wondered how many men had the privilege of seeing her stripped bare. She was a grown woman, sexy as hell. The number wasn't one or none. You won't be joining their ranks, let it go. But he couldn't let her go. She wound her way into his every thought, waking and not.

One of the organizers clapped her hands together noisily and announced the doors would be opening. He soaked up one more look at Beth and turned and stalked to the WECGA booth in the corner.

Go West was on one of the inner aisles, close to the end but in just far enough that he couldn't see her. In lulls of conversation, though, her laughter would carry and he'd find himself pacing a few steps into the crowd before reeling back.

In addition to Kent, he had two other people scheduled over the course of the day, overlapping schedules so he'd have time to network when there were two people at their booth. When Allison arrived, he took the first opportunity and walked the long way around the room. So he could pretend it was about saying hello to everyone and passing out business cards to new faces, but his destination wasn't back where he started.

He pulled up short of the Go West booth, though, because Beth was talking to an interested customer. Male. Tall. Very interested.

"Our tasting room is open every afternoon," he heard Beth murmur as she slid a brochure into the man's hands.

She was rewarded with a smile and a subtle lean from the stranger, which she saw and seemed to like, and a glower from Finn, which thankfully she didn't see because she wouldn't like.

Tough. He resumed his intercept course.

"Will you be the one pouring the wine?" Mr. Must Work Outside asked.

She smiled—smiled!—and shook her head with regret. "Not usually, no."

"If I give you my number, would you call me when you're behind the bar?"

She laughed. "You'd be waiting a while, I'm afraid. But our bartenders are all fantastic."

"Hmmm, that won't do. I'm not a patient man. How about a private tasting?"

Finn clenched his jaw tight enough his teeth protested and willed Beth to turn this douchebag down. His wish was denied. She fluttered her eyelashes and handed over a business card. "Tell you what…if you come by the winery, show the bartender my card. If I'm free, I'll make an exception for you."

Enough of that nonsense. Finn took the last few strides to bring him alongside Beth. He saw the moment she sensed his presence, her eyes got wide and she bit her lower lip. Damn straight.

CHAPTER SIX

Beth slid her best don't do this look at Finn but he wasn't having any of it.

He reached out and curved his hand gently around her elbow. "Can I talk to you for a minute?"

"I'm in the middle of something here," she muttered through a smile. And I won't feel guilty about it.

The man whose name she hadn't yet gotten—and didn't really want but would pretend to if it pissed Finn off, and how juvenile was that—nodded his head toward the exit. "Actually, I gotta go. But I'll call you." He glanced at the card, even though she'd introduced herself ninety seconds earlier. She definitely didn't want his name or number. "Nice to meet you, Beth."

She kept her pasted on smile in place until he turned away, then pursed her lips together and turned her attention back to the rude one. "Yes?"

He glanced behind her where she was pretty sure Gavin was flirting with a group of women. "Come with me."

"No." She stood her ground.

He cocked one eyebrow in silent challenge, then took another tack. "Please?"

She laughed despite herself. "You don't pull off requests very well."

He pressed against her upper arm, steering her toward the double doors leading out of the great room. He didn't leave any room between their bodies and in the small space between them he whispered, "What can I say? I like to be in charge."

That should not make her throb. It totally did. She decided the safest response was none at all. A "don't feed the wild animals" type of thing.

In the foyer he pointed down a hallway, then another. The dull roar of the crowd faded and all of a sudden they were alone.

Finn had asked—sort of—and she'd blindly followed him. She swallowed hard against whatever that might mean and tried to look business-like. "What did you want to talk about?"

He let her step away from him, just watching her as she put some space between them. He stretched the silence out long enough that she wondered if he might not answer. But then he did and made her see red. "Don't tell me you actually wanted that guy's number."

Screw him and the commitment-phobic horse he rode in on. "I want all the numbers, Finn. I'm a single woman in her thirties. I'm not going to apologize for looking for a mate."

He sneered and took a step closer, backing her up against the dark wood paneling. "I wouldn't advertise that too loudly. You wouldn't want to come off as desperate."

Beth couldn't hold back either the eye roll or the harsh laugh. Who was he kidding? "I don't feel desperate. I don't think that guy or any of the others have thought that about me, either. Only you and your committed bachelorhood, also known as baby phobia—"

He cut her off with a hard, angry kiss, his lower lip pushing against her teeth, practically forcing her to nip at him. She gasped instead, hungry for more. For his tongue and his silence, preferring this Finn to the pissed off hulk. So she welcomed him into her mouth and against her body, relishing the press her breasts against his chest and how their hips aligned just so. Oh how she ached to feel him inside her, not just pressed hot and hard into her belly. But even that tease was delicious, knowing that she did that to him.

No, jealousy did that to him. She told her inner voice of

reason to shut the hell up. She had a man to kiss. They were barely hidden in the side hall, nothing else was going to happen. Just a kiss.

One long, needy, awesome kiss.

When he pulled away, they were both breathing hard and their lips were wet and swollen. That was a priming for sex kind of kiss and she felt the effects of it from head to toe.

He dragged his hands up and down her sides. "What others?"

"Pardon?"

"You said that guy or any of the others."

"That's none of your business!"

"It sure as hell feels like my business." He dragged in a breath, then another, pulling himself back together. But he didn't let her go. As the slick mask fell into place, she braced herself for him to withdraw, but instead he buried his face in her neck.

She let her head fall back against the wall with a groan. "Don't...you can't get all possessive here. You aren't interested, remember?"

"That's not how I remember it at all." He slid one hand into her hair, tipping her face toward his. His eyes glittered with desire and it was hard not to succumb to the electricity between them.

"It's a package deal for me, Finn. Just because your kisses make me weak in the knees doesn't mean I'm going to throw away a few months of my life on an affair that can't go anywhere."

"Weak in the knees?" His normally hard mouth looked soft and inviting. Shiny and made for sex. He shifted, pressing his erection more deliberately into her core and she swallowed a moan. "My kisses do that to you?"

"I told you I like them," she breathed. "I obviously like them."

"Liking and being physically affected are two different things." He squeezed her neck with one hand and her hip with the other and pressed his forehead against hers. Their breath mingled together and Beth lazily thought that if they were surrounded by glass instead of dark wood and history, they'd have steamed up the space. "I know it makes me an asshole, but I like being under your skin."

She jerked under his grasp. "That does make you—"

"Because you're in my head," he muttered, continuing as if she hadn't sputtered a protest. "In my fucking bloodstream. Your scent is blueprinted on every cell in my body. Being close to you like this drives me mental."

It was all she'd ever wanted to hear from a man. She could weep from the near perfection except for the silent but that followed. But I'm not a forever man and I'll leave you before you snake your way into my heart. And if she were in his bloodstream, it wouldn't take long to send him running scared.

She wasn't playing that game. The words were heavy, refusing at first to be dragged out, but she managed to press her hand against his chest and shake her head. "I'm looking for someone to get serious with. Are you that guy?"

There was no honest answer to that question that wouldn't break her heart, but she ducked her head to find his gaze anyway. What she saw there took her breath away. Did he know how tortured he looked? And didn't that just make her heart heavier. Double damn.

He leaned in, slow enough for her to say no. She didn't. Couldn't. This kiss was bittersweet and lingered on the last beat. Another attempt at walking away. When he pulled away, he held her gaze, but the tortured look was gone, replaced with simple regret. "I don't want to lie to you."

Sadness spilled into her chest cavity, as if her heart sprang a leak. Maybe it did. Was it possible to love someone after a year of fighting and a few kisses? She steeled herself against wondering anymore about how they'd ended up like this. It didn't matter. "We need to stop doing this." She pressed her lips together, forcing them into a smile that didn't mean anything other than she didn't want to cry. Wouldn't fool anyone, but it didn't matter. "I need to go."

This time, she was the one to walk away.
And she didn't look back.

— —

He'd called himself a lot of names since succumbing to his attraction to Beth. Jackass. Bastard. World's Most Callous Man. But the truth was, he was an idiot.

Finn didn't head back into the hall right away. He just...couldn't. And he hated himself for being weak. He went out the side door instead but didn't get far before a light rain started. Cursing, he returned the way he came, but he couldn't bring himself to go inside. To watch Beth smile at customers. Hear her laugh.

He wished one of them would bend. You mean her. You want her to press pause on her biological clock so you can get your rocks off for a few months. It would be more than he'd given any other woman in a number of years, but it wasn't nearly enough.

Beth deserved forever. And he wasn't that man.

The door opened, thumping into his shoulder, but he didn't say anything. It barely registered.

"Sorry, man." A young kid, probably in his early twenties, stopped beside him and pulled a pack of cigarettes from his pocket. Finn was pretty sure there was no smoking allowed within a few metres of the entrance, but saying something would require saying something, and he didn't want to talk. To anyone.

Instead he grunted and shifted over a foot.

The rasp of the lighter, that first inhale. The tip of the cigarette glowing red with each inhale. Finn had smoked for a couple years in university. When he was young and felt invincible. It had never had the same calming effect on him that it did on others, but what the hell. Maybe it would sharpen his focus. Dull his hunger for what he couldn't have. "Can I bum one of those?"

The kid held out the paper carton, then the lighter.

Finn inhaled deeply, pulling the curl of smoke deep into his lungs. Not deep enough to reach the ache, but it was something.

College was also the last time he'd had what he'd call a broken heart. The irony wasn't lost on him. One nail in his coffin wasn't enough. Next he'd be binge drinking and singing R.E.M. songs like they held unique truths about his life.

There wasn't anything special about losing one's head over a girl. It was practically a cliche and Finn was better than that.

He took another drag, then held the smoke between his fingers until the kid went back inside. He ground the half-smoked cigarette under his foot then flicked the butt into a garbage can a few feet away.

He was stronger than that. And it hadn't done anything for the hunger.

— —

The rain persisted over the afternoon and heavy clouds brought a premature darkness as they wrapped up for the evening. Finn had stuck tight to his corner, and while he'd heard her voice a few times, had been spared having to watch Beth work. His luck ran out at the service entrance when she pulled up in her car just as he stepped outside. She popped her trunk and dashed through the heavy drops of rain to four large boxes stacked against the wall.

Keep going, his heart said.

He stopped. "Can I help?"

She froze for a second, then nodded with an apologetic smile. "Thanks."

They split the work, fitting two boxes in the backseat, one in her trunk and one on the passenger side.

"I didn't think this through," she shouted through the heavy patter of water on metal as they paused next to her door. "Thanks for your help."

He shrugged. Her hair was plastered to her head and her blouse clung to her shoulders and breasts like a second skin. Another stolen moment. He didn't feel put out in the least. He wanted to reach out and push the droplets off her nose, but he stuffed his hands in his pockets instead.

"You're getting soaked."

"I'm fine." He nodded to the boxes. "You going to be okay with those?"

"Yeah, I just need to drop them at the winery on my way home."

He looked up at the sky. "Maybe leave them in your car overnight. Take them tomorrow."

She winced. "It's foodstuff. Organic chips, that kind of thing. Ty will kill me if I don't properly store them at all times."

That didn't make any sense to Finn, but he shrugged. Not his problem.

She opened her door and reached halfway toward him, as if she was going to squeeze his arm, then changed her mind.

Touch me, he wanted to plead.

Weakling, his inner voice mocked.

He turned and stalked away.

— —

Beth realized Finn was following her when she hit the city outskirts. He lived in Windsor and had no reason to head in this direction at the end of a long day of work. She thought about calling him and telling him to turn around but, oh god, what if he wasn't actually following her. What if he was heading into the country for someone else, or for work. It was the height of ego to assume she was his motivation for anything given that she'd pushed him away repeatedly.

But as she took the Essex bypass and he continued to trail behind her, her heart did a little dance.

Off-limits, she reminded herself. No future. No babies,

no I love yous.

Her breasts didn't seem to care. They swelled heavy in her damp bra, nipples straining for more than the sporadic brush of her blouse. Her thighs were on board with damning the future too. They were positively vibrating at the thought of parting for Finn and all the pleasure he would surely bring to every part of her body.

The rain picked up again, heavy enough now for the fastest windshield wiper speed. She slowed down and willed her body not to distract her until they were safely at the winery. And then maybe she'd invite Finn back to her place.

What had he suggested the day of their first kiss? They had this chemistry between them. It was distracting. Maybe they needed to get it out of their system. Kissing hadn't done that.

Maybe they needed to excise all their demons in one fell swoop. One hot, sweaty, kinky swoop.

Maybe not kinky. Finn seemed like a lusty but vanilla type of guy. Which would be awesome too. She'd never been that dirty herself, except in her fantasies.

Where Finn may or may not have tied her up a few times.

Focus. Finally the quiet streetlights of Wardham appeared in the distance, and then they were driving through town. She turned left at the main intersection, unable to see the beach straight ahead now that dusk had fallen. But it was there. She drove past Kendall's Hardware and the pizza joint, then up the hill, curving around the bluffs before dropping again and carving closer to the lake. Up ahead an OPP cruiser was parked at the side of the road, a few metres shy of the entrance to the winery. She slowed down, wondering if something had happened, but the police officer inside the car had his head curved toward his computer. Glancing in the rearview mirror, she saw Finn was still with her.

If something happened, she wouldn't be alone when she found out. But that didn't stop a bubble of anxiety from lodging itself in her chest as she drove down the long lane to the modern main building but everything was dark and the parking lot empty. She parked right in front of the main doors and Finn did the same.

"You unlock. I'll bring these in," he yelled at her through the downpour. She already had the keys out. The sooner they got back to her place and out of the wet, the better.

She held the door as he brought in the four boxes, then together they moved them to the kitchen. She leaned against the stainless steel island for a minute, catching her breath. "Wow, that's quite the storm out there, eh?"

"You aren't mad that I followed you?" He moved closer but kept his hands to himself.

She shook her head slowly. It was hard to be sexy when one looked like a drowned rat. Want to come back to my place and share a hot shower? No strings attached, please disregard everything else I've ever told you? It sounded weak, even to her own ears. Before she could muster a better, hotter, more believable invitation, he was stepping back. Moving away. Shutting down.

No! But she didn't say it.

"I just wanted to make sure you got home safely." He tightened his lips and shoved his hands in his pockets. "It was probably a stupid idea."

"You were just being a friend." She willed her smile to reach her eyes but she didn't like the way he was looking at her without looking at her. It felt a hundred kinds of wrong.

He frowned slightly. "I didn't have anything else to do tonight. I'd do it for anyone."

Yeah. A hundred kinds of wrong. "We should go," she whispered.

"I'll follow you back to town. Make sure you get home okay." His voice was gruff but distant. She wanted him closer. Wanted his words rough and hot against her skin.

You don't always get what you want.

Another nod. That was all she had. It wasn't enough.

She locked up then got in her car without looking at him.

It was too hard wanting more than she knew was good for her. Or him for that matter.

She didn't get very far. At the end of the lane was a small lake of water, growing by the second. A rush of water told her the culvert on the other side of the road was overflowing. And on the other side of the road, where the OPP cruiser had been, red flares warned that the road was closed. Even if she could see in the other direction, she knew the dip in the road was deep enough that driving through the water wouldn't be safe. They were stranded.

A rap on her window told her Finn had also figured out their problem. He pointed back to the winery before disappearing again into the night. His car started up again, he did a three-point turn, and then she was alone with the lake and the rain and the crushing realization that she was going to be alone with Finn for an entire night. And not in the good way.

CHAPTER SEVEN

Finn stood brooding under the overhang as she silently unlocked for the second time in one night. Inside she pressed the alarm code and flipped on the light. Her wet shoes skidded a bit on the tile floor and her muscles screamed as she tensed to stay upright. God, she was tired. And soaked to the bone.

She glanced over at Finn. He'd dumped his briefcase on one of the benches and was scrolling through his phone. Not looking at her. Really not looking at her.

Two could play that game. She pulled out her phone and texted Ty. Think the road to the winery is closed. May be stranded here with Finn.

His response was swift. And crude. There are condoms in the bathroom off my office.

Her heart did not pick up at that thought. And also, ew. Glad you're concerned for my safety.

Are you okay?

Too little, too late.

Call me in the morning. Not too early.

Her lips quirked despite her fatigue and general grumpiness.

"Cancelling a date?"

Beth wasn't one to swear, but a big ol' F you was on the tip of her tongue as she looked over at Finn again. He was glaring at her, like it was her fault they were stranded. She squared her shoulders and smoothed out her facial expression. "You didn't need to follow me."

"Yeah, I did." He was wearing a black polo shirt and

dress pants, but as he crossed his arms his shirt glinted under the overhead lights. She wasn't the only one who needed dry clothes.

She let it go. The less they talked, the better. "Come on. Ty and Evan both have bathrooms in their offices. And couches. We can do Rock Paper Scissors for which of us gets Ty's office."

"It's all yours." His jaw twitched like he was mad she gave him a choice. Like he didn't want extraneous information just because she wouldn't have a fling with him. Whatever.

"You don't know what you're giving up," she said with an unnecessary amount of tease in her voice.

His jaw clenched and his eyes narrowed. "You don't think I know?"

Poor Finn, can't get laid without consequences. No. Won't get laid because he doesn't like the consequences. Again her inner twelve-year-old rolled her eyes.

"Ty has a TV and a computer hooked up as a media player. Probably a fully stocked bar fridge." She stomped past him and headed for the landing, tossing her last volley over her shoulder without glancing back. "I'm going to take a shower. I'll find you a change of clothes and put them in Evan's office for you."

— —

He watched Beth sway her hips up the stairs, struck dumb by the tantalizing image of her in a steamy shower. Hot water sluicing between her sudsy breasts, held in place by his hands as he pressed into her from behind. On his knees, spreading her pussy open and dying from the wonder of his first taste of her. Watching her recover from her orgasm, panting and slowly releasing her hold on his hair. Sliding down to kiss him, taste herself on his mouth, and then shove him back so she could return the favour. The sway of her ass in his blurry vision as he died and went to heaven.

Something he'd never actually experience.

He wanted another cigarette. Or a few rounds in a boxing ring.

The West brothers' offices were at the other end of the building from Beth's office and the boardroom he'd set up shop in when he worked here. Far enough away that he couldn't hear Beth once she disappeared down the shadowy hallway that snaked around the perimeter of the second story.

But he still felt the soft slide of fabric as she unbuttoned her clothes. Heard the hiss of hot water as if he was standing in the room watching her bathe. Felt her rejection as if he'd actually followed her and asked to join.

No, Finn. I want more than you can offer. I want everything.

He shook it off, checked the doors to make sure they were locked, and slowly followed her upstairs. When he got to the executive offices, he passed the closed door to Ty's office and walked straight to the end.

Finn liked Evan's office. Dark, modern, pristine. A large wooden desk dominated the room, but tucked against the wall closest to him was a black leather couch. Beth had set a pair of cargo shorts and a white Go West t-shirt there. She'd also turned on the light in the en suite bath, a fact that gave Finn an instant hard-on. You're pathetic. But it didn't feel pathetic as he stripped down to his boxers, stepped into the room, and heard the rush of water on the other side of the wall.

He turned his own shower on. The steam quickly lifted the day's work off his skin, the salty scent mingling with a mint body wash he found on the shelf. Next door, Beth turned off her water and he took his cock in hand.

Wet footprints on the tile. Stroke. An oversized towel wrapping around her skin, blotting it dry. Squeeze. He visualized each step of her post-shower ritual, the impossible nearness of her bringing him quickly to the edge. Smoothing moisturizer over her lush curves. Pump. Lifting the towel higher to work on her long, dark hair. Baring her bottom. Jerk.

With a strangled cry, Finn filled his hand, legs almost buckling in his release.

Heart pounding in his chest, he tried to make out what was happening on the other side of the wall. Had she heard him? Do you want her to know what you just did?

He took his time rinsing clean. It would be a long night, no need to rush toward more awkward silence. Maybe his laptop battery would last long enough to do some work.

He turned off the water. For once, working didn't appeal. Too bad what did appeal wasn't on the table.

A clean white towel hung just outside the shower. Had she put it there? As he scrubbed it over his skin, harder than he usually would, he thought of her hands on the fabric. Her hands on him. He snorted. He could play that cycle of fantasy and wanking off all night. It wouldn't satisfy his urge to be inside Beth. Nothing would. He pulled his boxer briefs back on and strode back into the main part of Evan's office, still towel drying his hair.

He didn't realize he wasn't alone until Beth cleared her throat.

He snapped his gaze to the doorway, where she leaned against the frame. Barefoot, damp hair, and touchable cotton, t-shirt and snug shorts, in between. He was doomed. "Sorry to interrupt," she said sweetly, and he suspected that was a lie. "I managed to scrounge up some dinner for us, if you're interested."

He should say no. He knew that was the right answer. The distancing, protecting both of them answer.

But the disappointment in her gaze as he dropped the towel to cover his midsection—the obvious loss of what she'd been enjoying—fed an ugly part of him that wanted to be wanted. On his own terms, as a man. Without any strings.

This was a winery and they were alone for the night. The dinner would surely involve opening a bottle or two. And he was a pathological charmer. He'd turn it on. Turn her on. Because he wouldn't be able to help himself.

She'd hate him for it.

But then she licked her lips as she lifted her gaze to his now bare shoulders and he made a new deal with the devil. One night, if she wanted. If she initiated. And damn the consequences.

"Sounds great. Let me just get dressed."

She made some quiet noises about being in Ty's office when he was ready and disappeared.

— —

She'd seen Finn almost naked and hadn't fainted. That was success of a sort. He really did have a perfect body. Broad shoulders, lean waist, powerful thighs. Strong, corded arms that could easily pick her up and toss her onto the nearest flat surface for ravishment. Dark hair dusting his tan skin in enough places to tease and tantalize. And was it possible that he was taller without his clothes on?

The picnic dinner she'd pulled together from the kitchen and Ty's bar fridge needed more wine. And she needed to dim the lights. Enough waffling. She was going to seduce Finn Howard. In all his naked glory.

As Ty had promised, there was an unopened box of condoms in a drawer in his bathroom. She left it there—no need to show her hand too early—and moved restlessly around the office. A movie. She fired up the TV and was navigating through the movie files Ty had pre-loaded onto his media player when Finn stepped silently through the door. She willed herself not to blush again. Most of his good bits were covered, but her imagination had more than enough fodder from earlier.

Wind and rain lashed the window, and she used that excuse to mumble about the weather while she scrolled through action movies. "How about The Avengers?"

He curved one eyebrow up at the nervous tone in her

voice. "You want to watch a movie?"

"You don't? He's got TV series as well—"

"Why don't we eat first?" He nodded to the food she'd spread out on the low coffee table.

Anticipation fluttered in her chest, but she needed something to fill the silence and mask the thud of her heart in her chest. "Do you want to open the wine while I find some music?"

A slow, seductive grin spread across his face. "That sounds nice."

God. Wine, food, music, and Finn. It sounded dangerous and delicious. Not nice. And from the look on his face he knew it. She slid her phone out of her bag and thumbed through her playlists. Most of her country music didn't feel right for Finn. Why didn't she know what he listened to? You don't know him that well. She frowned slightly. He was smart, urban, liked nice things…Well, let's see how he feels about Feist. She hit play and docked her phone on the stereo on the wall.

As the first strums of guitar music and strong female vocals surrounded them, Finn dropped to the floor and patted the space next to him. He'd uncorked a bottle of Riesling, but he waited until she was sitting to pour an ounce into her glass.

She smiled at the offer. "You don't want to have the first taste?"

Half a foot separated them, but as he twisted to look at her, biting his lip and searching her face with his dark eyes, that space vanished. "I wouldn't want to presume it was my right to taste."

Her breath caught in her throat and he extended his index finger just far enough to touch the base of her wine glass. Ever so slowly, he nudged the bowl up to rest on her bottom lip, then tipped, flooding her tongue with tangy, subtle sweetness. She rolled the wine around in her mouth before swallowing, and when she did he made an appreciative noise that made her thighs clench together.

"Your turn," she whispered, pouring him a similar serving. She offered him the glass, not trusting herself to actually help him drink, and again he offered her a wicked smile. Stop knowing so much. He swirled, sniffed and tasted, then refilled both their glasses.

She pointed around the table at what she'd found: prosciutto, a cheese plate, and some cherries from the kitchen; pretzels, olives, and chocolate truffles from Ty's kitchenette corner.

Finn looked around the space and Beth knew what he was thinking. It was more mini-apartment than office. Where Evan filled his suite with work, Ty used this space primarily for play when he wasn't making wine downstairs. He had a mini living room set up in the bulk of the space, leaving only a small corner for a workstation. She grinned and held up a pretzel. "His oddity works to our advantage when stranded!"

Finn leaned forward and snagged the pretzel between his teeth.

"Hey, no biting."

His eyes flared bright as he snapped it in two and swallowed. "You don't like biting?"

"You're full of double entendres tonight." She licked her lips and reached for an olive, sliding it into her mouth. His gaze followed and stuck there, his eyes growing more hooded as she took her time savouring the snack. When she finished, she leaned forward, licked her lips again and whispered against his cheek, "I love that burst of salt on my tongue."

He groaned and leaned forward, his upper arm pressing into the side of her breast as he crowded against the table. "Here," he said, his voice rough and heavy. He dangled a small piece of proscuitto in the air as he shifted back. This time the rub was more deliberate and it was her turn to groan. "Open up like a good girl."

She gasped at the simultaneous offence and turn on, and he took that opportunity to dance the smoky ham across her tongue. She giggled and went with it, wiggling her tongue in the air to capture the paper-thin ribbon of meat.

"That's more like it," he murmured. "Salty and silky at the same time."

She reached for her glass of wine and took a sip, watching him over the rim the whole time. "Delicious." She set her wine glass down and slowly leaned in. "We should talk about what happened earlier."

He traced the edge of her face with his index finger and smiled. "Us kissing? Or you telling me to stop?"

She swallowed hard. "I won't tell you to stop tonight."

He shook his head slowly. "Nothing's changed."

She laughed. "Everything's changed. We're stuck here all night and we're both…"

He wove his hand back into her hair, sending tiny, delicious electric shocks into her scalp and down her back. Tugging her closer, he licked her lower lip. "Both what?"

The wet stroke against her skin made her throb between the legs. "Distracted," she gasped. "And grumpy. Because we need—"

He nipped her lip, and as she groaned and shifted closer, pressing their upper bodies tight together in an erotic tangle, he licked his way to her neck. "Yes? What do we need?"

"Oh damn you, Finn." She shoved her way between him and the coffee table, straddling his thighs. He stared at her from under eyelids heavy with lust and between them his erection made a prominent tent in his shorts. She walked her fingertips up his chest. "You were right all along. We need to get this out of our system."

"Terrible idea." He skated his palms up her thighs to the edge of her shorts.

"The worst," she agreed as she spread her legs wider and arched her back. "Have a better one?"

"Having a little trouble thinking right now, I'll be honest with you." He held her gaze, filthy intentions blazing in his eyes, as he slid his hand into the leg of her shorts and teased the skin at the top of her thighs. "A gorgeous woman writhing on my lap has that effect on me."

"Happens to you often?" She heard the bite in her words and didn't care. They both knew they cared more than they should. That they'd be hurt by this in the end. It didn't change anything.

His hand stilled for a moment, then he curved up and over her thigh, jerking her core hard against his. "Never like this," he growled.

Fear fluttered like a moth in her chest and she shoved it down. "You're wearing too many clothes."

"Liked what you saw earlier?"

"You know I did."

"We should finish dinner."

"We can eat after."

He slid his hands under her shirt, teasing the bare skin at her waist, then higher on her back. "After what?"

"Finn Howard, do you like hearing me say dirty words?"

His hands tightened against her back, then scooped around to cup her bare breasts under her t-shirt. He grunted something incomprehensible that she still understood as an instruction to take it off, and as she tugged it up and over her head, he sucked first her left nipple into his mouth, then her right, leaving a wet trail of hunger across the valley between her breasts and making her slippery with need further south.

She whimpered as he loved her breasts with his mouth and hands, his thumbs working her nipples in ways that made her cry out and see stars.

"I like whatever you're offering," he rasped against her skin. "But yeah, I want to know what you want."

"I want another kiss." The wish surprised her even as she spoke it, but even though she'd meant to say something naughtier, he seemed to like it. He wrapped his arms around her and twisted, sliding her to the floor and rolling on top of her in one fluid motion, pausing just long enough to shuck his own shirt.

And then they were touching, skin-to-skin, and she was

wrapping her legs around his waist to deepen the embrace beyond just a kiss. But he still took his time, savouring her mouth, using his hands to lavish attention on her breasts and all the other skin he could touch.

Just when she thought she might scream if they didn't lose their bottoms, he twined his fingers into hers and tugged her hands up above her head. He held both wrists in one hand and traced the other down her torso, circling her navel before teasing at the waistband of her shorts. A nervous flutter started in her belly as he got closer to discovering she wasn't wearing any underwear. She'd pulled on her cotton exercise shorts after her shower with uncharacteristic glee, but now she wasn't sure about that call.

Any doubts quickly vanished as his fingertips reached the curls on her mound and he groaned. He breathed out her name and shifted closer still, his cock a hard brand of appreciation against her side.

"Now what do you want?" A husky demand she had no interest in denying.

"Touch me. I want your fingers inside me."

A fierce, wolfish smile was her first reward, and then his palm rolling over her clit was her second as his fingers parted her cleft and discovered just how ready she was. He slid through her desire, spiralling her wetness up and around her clit before sliding first one finger, then two and finally three into her core.

She whimpered and rocked against his hand, and he shifted to the side, stretching out beside her. She reached blindly between them, fumbling like a teenager for his cock, and he slipped his hand out of her shorts just long enough to help with his button before sliding back in with a groan.

She found him hard and straining against his boxer briefs and couldn't resist teasing him for a minute, dancing her palm over the head. He bucked his hips toward her and growled against her mouth, then broke their kiss.

"Damnit, woman." He hissed as she pulled away.

She was panting and breathless, but she wasn't ready to give up control yet. "Tell me what you want," she teased.

"Touch me. Wrap your hand around my cock or I'll spank you."

The image of that made her gush against his fingers and he rocked into her welcoming hand.

"Like that idea?"

"I like you," she whispered. And then they were done talking.

— —

Finn set the pace, stroking and teasing enough to keep her in that animalistic head space where writhing on the floor half-naked seemed like a really good idea, but he wasn't in a hurry to make her come. First he wanted her fully naked. Then he wanted to taste her. He wanted her to come with her legs clenched around his head, her hands pulling on his hair, and then he wanted to slide so far into her that she'd never forget him.

When she started clamping her thighs around his hand, wanting more but maybe being on the edge of too sensitive, he slowed his kisses and whispered for her to stand up.

She pushed up with nervous eagerness, like a new filly finding her legs, and he rewarded her with whispered praise.

"So beautiful, Beth," he said as he kissed her thighs. "Gorgeous," as he pulled down her shorts and pressed his face into the soft swell of her belly right above her mound. She shook under his hands and he rose to join her, tangling their hands and tongues and hearts, before tumbling backward onto the couch as she pushed him and took over.

"I want to eat you out," he whispered as she slid their sexes together, and he wondered when he'd lost his shorts and where the fuck they were because he needed the condom he'd stashed in the pocket and he needed it now.

"Inside me," she answered, and that was it. There was no more foreplay. He flipped her over, and she canted one knee high on the couch and slid one hand lazily between her legs as she watched him rear up, find his shorts and fumble for protection.

He felt ten feet tall as he loomed above her, taking in her curvy paleness and the dark curls obscuring her sex. Nothing had ever felt quite like this moment, knowing they'd be joined intimately, that he would fill her up. He shook at the realization that this was the one and only time he'd be inside Beth. He clenched his jaw and stifled that thought. Here, now. Man and woman. All that he was capable of, so he'd better make it good.

As she reached for him, as he let himself fall forward, bracing one hand by her head and the other cupping her ass, he realized it was already good.

It was perfect. And in the morning, it would be the most bittersweet memory.

— —

Beth rocked her hips, aching to feel him move. Wanting him to lose control because of her, but Finn held his ground, rock hard all over. Sweat dampened his back where she pressed her hands and faint tremors wracked his body.

"I need a minute," he muttered, and her heart cracked open. Her cocky man was just as affected as she was. He's not yours. But he was for the night, and like women had since time began, she held him to her breast and whispered in his ear, filling him with confidence before sending him off to war.

"We can do it again," she promised. "And again. I don't need to sleep tonight. I just need you. Please take me, Finn. I want you to fuck me into oblivion."

His eyes glittered as he curled himself over her body and started thrusting in and out. Even as he wavered on the edge of control he seemed to know what she liked and wanted more of, and as she loosened her vocal cords and let herself just feel, he sped up.

The head of his cock rocked against a spot inside her that made her eyes roll back it felt so good and she called out his name. So he did it again, thickening inside her as she clawed at his back and started writhing against him.

"Good?" He squeezed her hip and surged like a man on a mission.

"Oh god," she moaned. Good didn't even begin to describe what was happening inside her body.

"You there?" he asked, and she squeezed his ass, urging him on. He gasped her name and she responded in kind, and then he jerked twice in quick succession, spending himself, and she rubbed underneath him like a happy kitten. She kissed her way across his chest as his muscles unclenched, then tipped her face up for a kiss.

She wasn't expecting the confused look on his face. "What?"

"You didn't come."

She shrugged. "I don't always." Rarely, if ever, but he didn't need to know that. Except apparently he thought he did.

Breathing hard, he held himself over her for a minute, then cursed and moved to deal with the condom. He didn't go far, though, so neither did she, shifting just enough to go from wanton slut to seductive mistress. Or something like that. In reality, they both probably looked like hot sticky messes, but she didn't care.

Finn turned back to her and tugged silently on her hand, pulling her up and into his lap. He stroked her hip and cupped her neck, and gave her his absolutely sternest look. "You should have told me intercourse doesn't do it for you."

She couldn't help but laugh. "Oh, it does it for me. It just doesn't make me…you know."

He stroked her leg and glowered. "Making you come is not optional for me."

"That's weirdly nice and caveman-ish at the same time." She shrugged. "It's just not a part of sex for me."

"It is for me. I want to give you that."

"Well, too bad you don't have a magic penis," she whispered with good humour. She'd had this conversation before, although no one had ever been this persistent.

"True. But my fingers and tongue, on the other hand…" He nudged her thighs apart and traced her sex with his digits. "Okay, let me ask you this. Beth, do you want to come?"

The question sent a dark thrill through her core and she nodded.

"Then be a good girl and spread your legs for me. I'm feeling hungry."

Could her face get any redder? Or her hopes any higher? That fluttery feeling was back and she tipped her head back. Finn let her slide against the arm of the couch, staying beneath her as he started to tease her with his fingers, and it was only when her own hands started to work on her breasts that he growled and slid to the ground, burying his face where she was wet and needy.

He licked and sucked and fucked with his tongue, pausing here and there to fill her head with dirty thoughts and filthy promises she knew he wouldn't be able to keep beyond morning, but it didn't matter because he was delivering everything she'd ever imagined right then and there.

"Finn," she gasped, pulling at his head as he sucked her clit into his mouth, and he hummed.

Hummed.

And she died and went to heaven..

CHAPTER EIGHT

As she trembled her way down from what Finn hoped was the orgasm of her life, he stroked her legs and traced circles on her tummy. When she finally blinked in his direction, he grinned. "Hungry?"

She nodded, and he tugged her up against him. They finished their dinner, then finished each other again in the shower, using a condom Beth grabbed there and then another on the floor again before finally, reluctantly, dragging their clothes back on and falling asleep wrapped around each other.

He woke up a few times in the night, not used to having a warm weight covering half his body while he slept, but he just drifted far enough into consciousness to remember it was Beth. It felt right, sleeping with her in his arms, even on a couch.

As dawn broke, he forced himself to stay awake, to savour the feel of her against him. Because soon enough she'd shut down and push him away. It was the price he'd pay for falling in love when he wasn't capable of honouring all that meant.

At some point in the night, he'd admitted that's what had happened. And it didn't happen when they screwed, or even when they kissed. Finn traced back through all their fights, to the first time she told him off, her eyes blazing and lips pink, and decided that was probably the moment he fell in love with her.

He couldn't regret not doing anything about it sooner. He'd loved her for a year and that didn't change the fact he couldn't imagine sharing a life with her.

If he could, with anyone, it would be her. His chest ached at the thought of Beth finding someone else to marry. To make babies with. To love on her front porch in matching rocking chairs as they grew old together.

But as much as he cared for her, he still didn't want any of that. Because a gorgeous baby girl with dark curls and flashing eyes would grow up. Ballet class. Karate class. Swimming lessons. Tutoring. Camp. His chest tightened at the thought of the mounting expenses for a completely fictional child. His condo wouldn't be appropriate and it wasn't a good time to sell. Cold sweat trickled down his back at the thought of losing some of the equity he'd carefully built up.

His company, not yet formed, would disappear into the smoke of could-have-been.

No, he told himself resolutely. He didn't want any of that. Wouldn't think of Beth all round with child, or how she'd get to that state. It wasn't for him. She wasn't his.

He'd let her push him away.

It was for the best.

— —

She didn't want to wake up. Waking up meant morning and morning meant a return to friendship.

Her back was pressed into Finn's chest, but he still seemed to know she'd woken. He tensed for a minute, then kissed the top of her head and rubbed his hand up and down her arm. "More olives for breakfast?"

The casual question lanced pain through her chest. It was all so easy for him. He probably did this morning after thing all the time, had it down to a science. Well, she shouldn't be surprised. Time to be tough. She shook her head and laughed. "There are some muffins downstairs in the kitchen. And coffee."

She needed space. She curled up and off the couch, not

looking back at him, and headed straight for the bathroom. After some deep breaths and Zen thoughts, she freshened up and worked her hair into a reasonable looking braid. But when she stepped back into the office, it was empty. So much for worrying about putting on a brave face. No face required, apparently.

She didn't know what to feel. Anger? That wouldn't be fair, although the kernel of a good grump definitely sat in her gut. She settled on sadness. Life just wasn't fair sometimes, nothing to be done about that. She grabbed some cleaning supplies from under the bathroom sink and set about returning Ty's office to pre-debauchery state.

Her phone rang as she was folding up her wrinkled dress clothes from the previous day. She glanced at the display— Karen Miller-Reynolds calling her at seven in the morning could only mean one thing.

She answered the phone. "Let me guess."

"Everyone in town knows that you were stranded at the winery with Finn last night, yes." Karen laughed. "Ty told Evan, who told Evie, who called me, hoping Paul might have some information."

"About me and Finn?"

"About the road closure!" Karen sighed. "Although I'd like some details about you and Finn."

"Nothing interesting to share on either point, I'm afraid." Liar, liar, pants on fire.

"Really? Did you turn him down?"

Quite the opposite, in fact. "Why would that be the only reason nothing happened?"

"Because the man has the biggest crush on you. It would be cute if he was seventeen. Now it's just—you know, get on with it already."

"He does not." But the more she thought about it, the more that made sense. Oh, Finn. All the feelings he could barely handle. Of course he'd need some time to process the night before.

"He does not what?" Finn's rich voice asked from the

doorway, and she spun around.

Beth sucked in a sharp breath. "Karen? I gotta go." She pressed END and tossed her phone onto her purse.

He nodded in the general direction of the kitchen. "I put coffee on."

"Oh."

"Did you think I'd gone?"

She flushed. "Maybe."

"Hey," he said softly, closing the gap between them and pulling her into his arms.

"I would have understood if you'd gone." She offered a weak smile.

"I wouldn't do that to you." He winced. "I'm sorry I gave you the impression I would."

She put on her best it's cool face. "I'm just not...this is my first one-night stand, really. I'm not experienced at the morning after thing."

His voice was sharp and edged with protest. "It wasn't a one-night stand."

But it was, and no amount of feeling would change that. All of a sudden her brave facade crumbled and she was trying in vain to blink back tears.

"I'm sorry," he said gruffly, and she shook her head. She was getting his shirt wet but it didn't matter. It was the shirt she'd lent him. He'd never wear it again. It wasn't him. He was oxford blue and dry clean only. This was just a dream. It didn't matter that she was losing it. He go home and change and be done with her.

"Nothing to be sorry for," she whispered. "I knew what I was getting. I wanted it. I wanted you."

"You deserve so much more than me." He swallowed hard, his Adam's apple bobbing against her head, and she wanted to cry out that he deserved more, but that wasn't her fight. He'd need to figure out on his own that love didn't demand or force change. That she could be a part of his life without taking it over.

But that still wouldn't matter, because at some point

they'd fight about the next step. Rings. Weddings. Babies.

And it wouldn't be the good kind of fight.

It would be this, but ten times worse. A hundred times. Because then the fact that she loved him wouldn't be a secret and she couldn't harbour a secret hope that he might change his mind.

Which she did. Despite all signs to the contrary—his resigned expression as he dried her tears and made her coffee, his gentle kiss after packing up his bag, and the resolute way he left without looking back—despite all of that, she thought he might just change his mind.

She was a fool.

— —

It took Beth nineteen days and two painfully polite meetings to realize Finn wasn't going to come back to her. Wasn't going to realize that love was a precious gift, not a threat. He really was a confirmed bachelor, no matter what, and her heart truly was broken. No white knight was going to mend it.

So she put her Lilith Fair CDs on repeat and started crying.

Unfortunately for Ty, it was at the end of the day when everyone else had left, and he just happened to walk past her office as she tossed used tissue after used tissue aimlessly onto the floor. And it was his tough luck he stepped inside and asked what was wrong.

Instead of answering, she grabbed his hand and dragged him down to the bar, snagged two bottles of wine—not the Riesling as she was sure she'd never drink that again—and held one out in his direction.

Ty, being Ty, didn't ask any questions. He just opened the wine and took a big drink. "Who's the asshole?"

"Finn."

"Fuck him."

And that was pretty much the agenda for the next hour.

At some point, Beth wanted to dance, so they ended up in the great hall, and that's where Evan found them.

"What are we doing?" He strode toward them, unbuttoning his jacket, and Beth hiccuped as she started giggling.

Ty waved his bottle of wine at his brother. "Getting drunk and talking about how much men suck."

Evan cocked one eyebrow. "I'm not sure I'm game."

"Come on, it's for Bethie."

"Don't call me that," she threatened, but with the blurry double vision she had going on, she might have been talking to a chair.

"Don't you have girlfriends for this?" Evan sank to the floor next to her and tugged her close. "Evie's always up for a girls' night."

"I asked her. She invited me over to her place, but Liam is out and she's got all three kids tonight, so that sounded…" She wrinkled her nose. "Noisy."

"You're noisy."

"I wouldn't want to have to filter."

"Ahhh." Evan sighed. "So Finn's a jerk?"

"Whatever, I don't even like him."

"You love him."

"I hate him."

Ty laughed. "I think, princess, it's possible that what you and Finn have is beyond love and hate."

"We don't have anything," she wailed and reached for her bottle of wine again, but Evan moved it out of reach.

He shook his head. "You're cut off."

"You're just as bad as he is," she muttered. "What is it with you guys? Scared of commitment. Jerks."

"Should I fire him?"

"Yes." Beth hiccuped again.

"It'd be a real shame to lose his insight. He's got a good vision for what we need and he's cheap."

Beth shook her head. "That doesn't sound like Finn. Except the good vision part. I suppose."

Evan shrugged. "His last invoice was half the amount I was expecting."

She stilled. "Why would he do that? And why didn't I see it?"

"He sent it directly to me." Evan smoothed her hair. "Come on, I'll drive you home."

She shook her head. "Maybe he realized his advice was crap." The brothers laughed. "No, I'm serious! I'm going to call him."

She clambered to her feet and headed upstairs. Behind her Evan and Ty made some muttering noises but neither stopped her. Maybe they followed. Maybe they didn't. She didn't care.

She wasn't calling Finn on a personal matter. This was business. So she used her desk phone. It took three rings for him to answer.

"Finn Howard."

"Finn. It's Beth."

He paused and her chest ached. No. Business.

"I'm calling about your most recent invoice."

"I sent that to Evan." He sighed. "Beth, I'm sorry I haven't called."

"You have called, twice. I got both messages. Listen, about the invoice—"

"I mean, I should have called you as a friend."

"We're not friends."

Another long silence. "I suppose I deserve that."

This was not going as she planned. "About your bill."

"I don't want to talk about the invoice," he said, his words straining even over the phone line. "We haven't had a chance…I want to talk about you. How are you?"

She laughed, a hysterical watery burst of noise. "I'm fantastic. And that is not why I called so if we could return to the business at hand, that would be swell."

"Swell?"

"Indeed. Now, about your invoice. It was less than we expected."

"Not usually something people complain about."

"Well, I'm complaining."

"About my invoice?"

"Yes, the invoice. What else would I be complaining about?"

"Maybe that I've been a jerk?" He'd lost the sharp edge and his voice was now low and smooth, like he was managing her. She didn't want to be managed. She wanted to be loved but that wasn't on the fucking table.

"I definitely don't want to talk about that." *I don't want it to be true. I don't want you to be okay with being such a colossal idiot.* "I've just come from a business meeting with the executives of my organization and there was some discussion—"

"Exec—Beth, are you okay?"

"'Course I'm okay. I'm grrrreat!"

Another long pause. "Is it possible that you're drunk?"

Damn, she'd thought she'd managed her slurring better than that. "Define drunk."

"Are you alone?"

She glanced around her office. "At the moment, yes. Evan and Ty are around. We were talking about you before. It wasn't good."

"I can imagine."

"Stop that. Stop taking my hate on the chin." She shoved her hand over her mouth to keep from saying the rest. *Stop pretending my hate is almost as good as my love.*

"You want me to fight back?"

She didn't have an answer, so instead of responding she turned to her computer and opened an email he'd sent the day before with artwork for the new ad campaign. "I don't like the new art direction."

"Maybe we should talk about that when you've sobered up."

"No, I want to talk about it now. I don't like it. You don't get our brand at all."

"Tell me more about that."

"Shut up. Don't manage me." She propped her elbows on her desk and stabbed a finger at the computer screen. "This new stuff screams hipster yuppie bullshit."

"Hipster and yuppie at the same time? Aren't those a few generations apart? We were going for sophisticated and youthful. No funny glasses or minivans."

"We have a sense of community, Finn. Mr. Solitude. Mr. Wanna Be Alone Forever. S'okay, you don't get that. Whatever. But that's what we are, and this isn't it."

"This?"

"The artwork!"

"Right." But he said it like he knew they weren't talking about the artwork and that made her mad. Unfortunately, it also made her slightly nauseous. Fighting took too much energy when it wasn't what she really wanted to do. He talked quietly in her ear about market segments and branding, but she wasn't listening. Not to his words. Instead she let his voice wash over her, wiping away the bitterness. So sad to only get this small piece of him, but why was she hammering at him when he was putting up with her drunken phone call? Humouring her attack on his work when they both knew it was a rail against his cold, unfeeling heart.

No. Not unfeeling. Just unavailable. For his own reasons that he defended with appropriate boundaries. She was the one who couldn't keep it together.

"Finn?" She interrupted him with unexpected sobriety. "I have to go. I'm sorry to bother you. We can discuss this another time."

She hung up the phone with what she intended to be gusto but was probably more like a panicky flourish. Either way, she hadn't waited for his answer. She'd been told enough times.

He wasn't interested. It was time to let him go.

CHAPTER NINE

Finn had handled two in-person meetings with Beth just fine. Watched her across the conference table, hair smooth and face fixed in a polite mask, and convinced himself he'd get over her. Shame she didn't want a longer fling, but he'd survive.

The joke was on him.

One drunken phone call and he'd been ready to drive into Wardham and toss her over his shoulder. Screw her life plan. She missed him and he needed her. It was selfish and cruel and he didn't care.

Except he did care, a little too much, and it was that itchy worry that kept him away.

He didn't stay away because he was a good guy. He was most definitely not a good guy. If he thought he could convince her to keep him in her bed for a few months, he would. It was the terrifying possibility that she might be the one to convince him—into marriage, babies, and a stab at forever—that kept him glued to the ground.

She'd called on Thursday. On Friday, he tried to work and failed miserably. By Saturday, he was desperate for some time in the ring. His brother Ryan was visiting for the weekend, staying at their parents' place, and he called over there hoping to drag Ryan to the gym. Instead, the bastard roped him into an early afternoon of golf with their father and both of their brothers-in-law. He only made it through five holes before he feigned a work call and sent them on ahead.

He skipped dinner but he wasn't surprised when Ryan

called from the parking lot and told him to either buzz him in or come down to get his ass kicked.

"What the hell, man?" Finn asked as he swung the door to his apartment open.

"Janine told me you've been in a funk about a woman. That was new and different and rather improbable, so I thought I'd come over and get the dirt straight from you." Ryan kicked off his shoes and made himself comfortable on the couch. "Want to watch a game?"

"So by get the dirt, do you mean you're here hiding from your wife and kids?" Finn kicked his brother's feet off the coffee table, not caring to be gentle about it.

Ryan responded with a hard look. "That's uncalled for."

"You came here, remember? Knowing I'm in a pissy mood. Feel free to leave."

Another glare. "You're such an asshole."

"Takes one to know one."

"No fucking kidding." Ryan sighed. "Lynn's started smoking pot again."

"Jeez." Finn didn't feel strongly about marijuana one way or the other, but in addition to being a full-time paramedic, his brother was also in the Army reserves. He took his drug-free status seriously, and his wife's social usage had been an ongoing issue in their marriage. "Sorry, man. I didn't mean—"

"Yeah, you did. And you were right. Not about the kids, but…"

Finn felt like he owed his brother something after that. "You want a beer? Let me tell you about a girl I could've had."

— —

Monday he got a text summoning him to Sienna's house, but he knew the command request came from Janine. Finn thought seriously about ignoring it, but the last thing he wanted was for her to show up at his apartment, four kids in tow. The fingerprints threat alone made him shudder. And the boys would want to wrestle. No, he'd go, let her have her say, play with the kids, then pick up some seriously spicy Indian food for a very adult dinner. Alone.

She started almost as soon as he settled in front of the veggies and dip on the kitchen table.

"I've never known you to be afraid to go for something you want."

He shot her a warning look. This wasn't any of her business. Fuck. He didn't even want it to be his business. "I'm not afraid of anything."

"Oh, shut up. You're afraid of turning into our father." She couldn't have shocked him more if she'd actually shoved a metal rod up his spine—or made him sit up any straighter. She leaned in, holding his gaze for a silent minute before continuing. "Times are different now. You're a different person."

He moved his tongue around his mouth, all of a sudden parched beyond belief. He loved his sister. How could he tell her it wasn't just their father's life he didn't want? It was hers, too, and that wasn't in the past. That was here and now, a real and scary mess. He couldn't say that. Wouldn't hurt her when she'd already borne too many cuts from others. But nothing she could say would convince him to take even one step down a path that ended in bitter regret. Ryan, too. Probably Sienna and Kath once the bloom fell off the rose of their newer marriages.

The back door slammed shut and Sienna hustled in holding her youngest on her hip. She took one look at her older siblings, grabbed a pack of juice boxes, and sent the toddler back outside before pouring a round of lemonade. Finn took the proffered glass roughly, barely noticing the tangy sweetness as he swallowed a large mouthful.

"Are we having an intervention?" Sienna smiled at his scowl and leaned against the counter next to Janine.

"No," he said as the same time Janine answered yes.

"Is this about Finn's broken heart or his love-hate

relationship with the rest of us?"

He glared at his second youngest sister, twelve years his junior. "I don't have a broken heart. And I just love you, although the hate has a growing appeal."

"We worry about you."

"Because I'm all alone? Not necessary."

"No, because you're sad and bitter." She held up her hand as he opened his mouth to argue. "Let me reiterate—we're worried about you. Those words come from a place of love."

He snorted. "Thanks for the concern. And the drink. I'm going to be fine."

She nodded. "Of course you will."

"I like my life."

"Of course you do." Her tone was a hair this side of mocking, but he didn't push back because he was too busy wrestling with an unexpected question…did he?

He did. Of course he liked his life. He…his mind went blank. He had liked his life. Solitude had always been preferable to the mayhem his family chose.

"Ryan told me you're quitting your job." Sienna continued to press in that endlessly patient way she had, honed from dealing with toddlers all the time. "Why don't you move to Toronto or Chicago or New York?" Why hadn't he moved when he lost the radio gig? He was starting to think that just maybe his baby sisters knew him better than he knew himself. He wasn't at all comfortable with that possibility.

"It's easier to build my own business here," he intoned.

"You've never wanted to be the big fish in the little pond."

He shoved to his feet. "I'm not staying here for her."

In his peripheral vision his sisters exchanged knowing glances, and he realized too late that he'd shared too much information. As one, they rose and put their hands on their hips.

"You love her." Sienna said the words slowly, testing

them out. They'd never been said before about Finn and a woman.

"I misspoke," he muttered.

Janine pulled out her phone and sent off a quick text message, probably to Kath, and Finn shoved his hands into hair to keep from grabbing the phone and winging it across the room. She smirked, as if to say, you're stuck with us.

"That wasn't what I was thinking, although that's better. Healthier." Sienna coated her words with fine spun sugar. "You were staying here for us, which we never wanted or asked for, but we definitely appreciated. You might be a jerk to us but you're a great uncle."

Janine wasn't nearly as sweet. "Kind of a jackass move, pretending you didn't like us all those years."

He stalked to the large bay window overlooking the backyard and the six boisterous children playing in and around the sandbox. The houses in this neighbourhood were small and tired but well suited to a young family. That thought still caused him to break out in phantom hives, but he understood his sisters' choices better. "Kath on her way over?"

"After her midwife's appointment." Janine stepped beside him and leaned her head on his shoulder. "I know you probably want space right now. That's just not the Howard way."

He didn't want space, though. He just couldn't be sure that what he thought he wanted—Beth, constantly—would be what he wanted for the rest of his life.

So he opened up his crusty shell and spilled his heart out to his sisters. They poured more lemonade and cookies and let him rant and rave, and they didn't once point to the swear jar when he used all the adult words he knew to describe himself and the situation.

"I don't really get the big deal," Janine said when he finally took a pause.

Prickly discomfort crawled up his back. No one understood. No one except Beth, who'd been pissed off but accepted his boundaries without judgement.

"What if I can't be everything she needs?"

"Do you think John ever asked that about himself? I know what it's like to be married to a selfish bastard, and you aren't that. You'll be a handful but it will be worth it to her. That you want the very best for her makes you one in a million, Finn. And jeez, give the woman some credit to manage her own happiness. You won't make or break her. Give her your love and together you'll figure out the rest." Janine took a deep breath. She wasn't done. He'd had no idea his sister had this fire in her. She was far from broken. "Not all marriages work out. That's a hard reality of life. But the ones that do are magical."

"You still think that? Even after John left you?" He couldn't hold the skepticism out of his voice.

She laughed. "Obviously, mine missed some magic. But I got four amazing kids out of it and I'm still young. Every single day I wake up with my health and my future before me. I have an amazingly supportive family—and maybe I've relied on them a bit much of late—but I can manage on my own. I can thrive on my own. I can be happy on my own. But I don't want to. I want to find someone to share my life with. You've found that person, what are you waiting for?"

Wasn't that the million dollar question?

And that meant he needed to ask another question. The question. He wanted to do it right. He went from his sister's house to the mall but none of the jewelry stores there had what he was looking for, not exactly. Some rings were too busy, others too small. At home he started researching online purchases. With expedited shipping he could have exactly what he wanted by the end of the week.

The next morning he woke up invigorated and threw himself into work with renewed purpose. He showered, dressed in his favourite dark grey suit and red tie, and made some phone calls. The third one paid off in a big way. He booked a last-minute flight to Toronto and spent twenty-four hours pressing flesh and making deals. He made time before he left to stop by the ad agency that had done up the latest Go West campaign. He had a new idea he wanted them to get just right.

By Thursday he was home again. When the courier called up from the lobby at four in the afternoon, it took all of his willpower not to drive straight to Wardham and just ask her with the ring.

But the artwork would be done on Friday. They'd promised to rush. He could wait. They'd have the rest of their lives together and he wanted her to know just how serious he was about that promise.

CHAPTER TEN

It had been such a long, lonely week. After grabbing a bottle of Pinot Noir from the tasting room, Beth stopped at Wardham Grocery on her way home and picked up some beef strips, onions and peppers for a stir-fry. Why wasn't food sold in solo quantities? She'd have leftovers for the entire weekend at this rate.

She ran into Carrie and Ian Nixon on the way out. Ian had their son Drew up on his shoulders and Carrie was holding hands with their daughter Kaylie. They invited her out to their farm for fireworks on Canada Day. She stomped on the little green monster in her gut and promised she'd be there. Everyone else would be there as well—Evie and Liam with their three kids, Karen and Paul and their daughter. Even Ian's brother Kyle and his fiancée Laney would be in town for the holiday weekend. Everyone paired up. Except for Beth.

"You could bring someone," Carried offered. "Or I could invite a single friend?"

"Oh no, please don't do that." The thought of dating someone else turned her gut to lead. Being intimate with another man after Finn had made love to her…no, that wasn't going to happen anytime soon. "I have a friend I can bring if I don't feel like being a third wheel. Or—" she counted off on her fingers with a wry chuckle. "A ninth wheel."

Carrie squeezed her hand. "Just come by yourself. The kids are so demanding it's not like we're all couple-y all the time."

Except they were. In little moments, like Ian rubbing the small of Carrie's back even as he made truck noises with Drew. Or how Paul would search the entire room for Karen, as if she was only thing worth seeing sometimes. There was no avoiding that around her friends. They were all blessed with extraordinary love.

"I'll be there." She thought about her options as she headed home. As she put the food away, she made a decision.

He answered on the second ring. "Beth! This is a surprise."

"Hi, Peter." They exchanged pleasantries, then she dove in. "Listen, I'm calling because I'd like to invite you to some fireworks next week. Canada Day party at a friend's place in the country. Not a date, just as friends. If you don't already have plans. And if you get a better offer, you should take it, because as I say all of this out loud I realize it's not a very good one."

Peter laughed. "It's a perfectly decent offer between friends. Sure, if I don't get swept off my feet by a hot blonde between now and next weekend, I'd love to go with you."

Relief thumped hard in her chest. "Great." She glanced at the fridge. "Hey, listen, if you don't have plans for dinner tonight…"

— —

One glitch in Finn's plan was that he didn't actually know Beth's address. He knew she lived in the townhouse development on the west end of Wardham, on Beach Road, but there were forty units in the complex. As soon as the new artwork arrived, too late on Friday for him to find her at the winery, he called Evan.

"And why exactly should I give you her address?" The elder West brother had always been friendly to Finn, but this wasn't business, and his voice held no trace of kindness.

Finn was smart enough to realize he wasn't going to

charm his way through this conversation. "Because I love her."

"You should have realized that three weeks ago."

"Yep, but I'm slow." He waited for the panic to set in as he moved into the next admission but it didn't come. How about that? "I spent the week ring shopping."

"That's cocky."

"I'm willing to gamble. And next week I'm going to have a new ad campaign to show you."

Evan grunted. "I don't want you to change our marketing strategy for Beth. Your instincts are better than hers when it comes to this. That's just a business decision."

"This is better, I promise you."

Evan didn't sound impressed on that front but Finn would tackle that battle later. He had her address, that's all that mattered.

The first pair of visitor parking spots was full, so Finn parked further down the row of houses and walked back to Beth's place. Some of her neighbours had potted flowers out front. Beth had an evergreen topiary. Sleek and beautiful, just like her.

He rang the doorbell and stepped back. He wanted to remember every moment of this night and recount it regularly to their grandchildren.

She opened the door quickly and froze at the sight of him. "Finn!"

"Surprise." He grinned. She looked fantastic. She was wearing a red wrap dress and no shoes, her toes painted a matching cherry colour. He had a sudden vision of her in a bubble bath, waving those toes at him as she invited him to join her. Fuck, yeah. This felt right. "Can I come in?"

She glanced back into the house. "Uhm, sure. Yes, of course. Come in."

He followed her inside, but not very far before she stopped and turned around. "What brings you here?"

— —

God, he looked good. She drank in the sight of him. Dark jeans, white shirt, navy blazer. He held a folder and her gaze got stuck on his hands. Big, strong hands, dark hair hinting out from the cuff of his shirt. Short nails trimmed neatly at the end of long, thick fingers. Fingers that had teased and traced her sex, made her crazy and shattered her into a million pieces of happiness. Right before he just shattered her, and now he was in her house on a Friday night. Because of work.

He lifted the shiny folder in the air. "I brought a new ad design for you to look at."

"It couldn't wait until Monday?" Screw him. "I have a guest over for dinner."

That shit-eating grin dropped off his face. Good. "Oh."

"You remember Peter." She flipped her hair and planted her hands on her hips. "We're just having a glass of wine while I get dinner ready."

"Peter. From the park." Finn did something, a weird muscle tensing thing that made him look even bigger than normal, then strode past her into the kitchen. She gasped and scrambled after him, getting there just in time to see Finn point a finger at Peter's wine glass. Well, that was better than throwing a punch.

"How much have you had to drink, Pete?"

"It's Peter, actually, and we'd just opened the bottle, so—"

"Great, so you can drive. Time to go."

"Finn!" Beth yanked on his arm, pulling his attention back to her. "You can't kick my guest out."

"Do you want him here when I'm grovelling?"

That was not what she expected him to say. "Grovelling?"

"Begging for you to take me back? Making a fool of myself? Which you're going to love, so then there will be some kissing, which will lead to—"

She held up her hand. "I get the picture," she hissed. "So

let me get this straight—you're not interested in a relationship until you see me with someone else? Because that's pretty fucked up."

Behind Finn, glass clinked on her granite counter. "I'm going to go anyway," Peter said with a trace of laughter in his voice. "You guys seem like you've got some stuff to work out."

She stepped into his path. "No, stay. Please. Finn will go—"

"Finn will not go," the oaf said, referring to himself in the third person. "Finn has a lady to win back and doesn't really care at this point if there's an audience or not."

"Stop it." She turned and pleaded. "We can…I don't know. Why don't we have coffee tomorrow or something? This is all just a bit much. I've had a brutal week."

His eyes softened and he stepped closer to brush his hand over her cheek. "You've had a bad week?"

"It's a long story."

"I've got all the time in the world."

Peter cleared his throat and muttered a goodbye. This time she didn't try to stop him. When the front door clicked shut, she wearily moved away from Finn in search of her wine glass. "Show me what you brought."

He silently handed over the folder. Inside was a new take on the campaign targeting 30-somethings. It took her breath away. Couples. Sexy, passionate couples. Gay, straight, inter-racial, young and old. All tied together with a dark, seductive branding that she could almost taste it was so perfect.

He came up behind her, his chest hard and strong against her back, and he traced her earlobe with his lips before whispering. "I hope we captured it."

"What?" she breathed.

"Your community. With a marketing twist, of course."

She allowed a weak laugh. "Of course. It's fantastic."

"I'll present the whole thing to Evan next week but I wanted you to see it first."

"Thank you." She held her thoughts at that small

whisper, not wanting to break the spell of the moment with all the questions spiralling through her head and her heart.

"That's just the start." His voice was low and rough and oh so hot, she had a hard time not reading erotic promise in his tone and his words. "Now for the grovelling."

"No, Finn, don't." A dam broke and she couldn't bite her tongue any longer. "I've missed you so much and I desperately want you to stay. For the evening and for the night if you want. But I'm fragile here and I don't know if I want to hear…"

He turned her around in his arms and took her mouth. His kiss was firm and deliberate, confident that she'd bow to his will. And she would, oh boy would she, but first she wanted to ground whatever it was they were going to do in some reality.

She slid her hands between them, relishing for a moment the firm ridges of his body under the fine weave of the dress shirt before pressing them apart. "I'm not a fool, Finn. A woman can't change a man into what she wants him to be."

He gripped her shoulders. "But a man can change. Just a bit, just enough. With the right motivation."

"There's no motivation in the world that can convince you of the value of a white picket fence and two point five kids."

"I want you." He kissed her again, proving his point. She sighed and kissed her way along his jaw. She'd missed this, being close to him. Missed his smell and his hard, enveloping warmth.

But it would be even harder to let him go months down the road. "You want me, just me?"

"Why isn't that what you want to hear?"

"Because you wanting me means I'm the one that needs to change. Accept a half-life."

"Would loving me really not be enough?" Didn't he know that she already did? She knew how hard it would be to walk away from the love of her life. She didn't need to guess at that pain.

"It would. Oh Finn, of course it would. For a while. But in time I'd come to resent you, and that love would turn to hate. I've hated you before—"

"You never hated me."

She allowed a half-smile. "No, I suppose I didn't."

He tugged her closer and drifted a sweet kiss over her forehead. All the passion they'd shared, and that scant touch undid her. Hot tears threatened her lower lids and she closed her eyes in protest. No, she wouldn't cry. Wouldn't be weak in this moment when she needed to be strong for herself.

"I could tell you I want a minivan full of kids, soccer balls and popsicle sticks littering the floor. I'm a half-decent salesman, I could make you believe it, too." His regret was palpable. She should appreciate his honesty, but at the moment, it was hard to focus on anything besides the giant knot in her throat. "But that isn't the future I see."

"I know," she whispered. "It's okay." It would be, someday.

"If our kids play soccer, they need to go to practice in your car."

She pressed her lips together and swallowed back a sob. He needed to stop talking, stop caressing her arm. She needed to get away from him and— "What?"

He laughed, and she pushed hard against his chest.

"Finn, that's not funny. That's actually an incredibly asshat thing to say to me." She scrambled away from him, fury shaking every cell in her body. "I'm trying to be the bigger person here, let you live your stupid, empty, childless life, and you're making fun of me."

"Well, we can't very well rectify that if you're standing all the way over there."

"Rectify what?"

"The childless thing." He took off his blazer and tossed it halfway across the room, his broad shoulders bunching and stretching his shirtfront as he did it. She gaped at him, still trying to process what was going on as he popped the first button on his shirt, then the second. The thin dusting of dark curls she loved to tangle her fingers in sprang into view, then his washboard stomach.

"What are you doing?" She pressed the flat of her palm to her belly. Now was not the time to get turned on by Finn stripping. Oh god, not the belt.

"Getting naked."

"Why?"

"Because we're having some communication difficulties, and I want you to see just how serious I am about making babies with you."

Whoa. "I think I missed something."

"Two kids. I've done the research, I can't fit three across the backseat of my car. And I'm not trading it in."

"Research?"

"You should probably stop talking and take off your dress."

"Why?"

"Dress. Off." He didn't wait for her to comply. Two big strides and he was across the room. He slid one finger along the v-neck of her wrap dress and with the other hand started working at the belt tie.

"Finn, stop." She wrapped her hands around his wrists. "I don't want to make a baby today. This is crazy."

He stroked his hands around her waist and pulled her hard against him. "That's our deal. You make me crazy. And I love you."

"You love me." She whispered the words, then laughed at the absurdity of the situation. "I love you too, but—"

"No buts. I love you, I want you, and whenever you're ready, I want to plant a baby in you. And then another, if you're game. There won't be any drink boxes in my car and crayons will be very carefully monitored—"

"By you?"

"By me. My neuroses are my own. I won't make them yours."

"I'll monitor crayons for you." The tears she'd been holding back now slid down her face and she tipped her head back and laughed. "I'll buy stock in wet wipes and Mr. Clean Magic Erasers."

"You like the ad campaign?"

"I love it." She laughed as she cried. "Pass the folder over, I want to look at it again."

He shook his head. "In a minute. I have something else to run past you first." He thumbed away a teardrop and kissed her cheek.

She wiped her face with the backs of her hands. "I think I like the idea of getting naked better."

He grinned. "This will be worth it. And then we're definitely getting naked. You had a bad week?"

"Finn, you're giving me conversation whiplash." She stroked his chest. "It's getting better, anyway."

He kissed her again, this time more hungrily, and she lost herself in the taste of him. He licked her lower lip as he eased back, sending a shiver down her spine. "Okay, one last thing. Dinner with Peter tonight, what was that all about?"

"Just friends, I promise. I was…lonely, and I bought enough food for an army, and he was the only person I could think of that might be free."

His face fell. "Shit. I'm sorry, my girl."

"You're here now, that's all that matters. Hey, do you want to go to Canada Day party with me? Fireworks on a farm out in the country. Carrie Nixon's husband is organizing."

"Sure." He smiled down at her, pure indulgence written on his face. She laughed at the insanity of it. "What?"

"You want babies?"

"I want you to have my babies. Yeah." He nudged his erection into her belly. "I'm hard just thinking about it."

"Holy crap."

"But you're right, today isn't the day for that. We can get started on that in a few weeks maybe. First…"

He took a step back and she bit her lip at the glory of her man. Tall, broad, strong and utterly in love with her. He stood before her naked from the waist up, silky dark hair swirling on his chest and forearms. Muscles dipping here and there, begging for her tongue. She moved toward him but he held up one hand as he dug in his pocket with the other. It wasn't until he pulled something sparkly out and twirled it on his finger before sinking to one knee with a cocky-as-all-get-out grin that she realized what he was doing.

"You didn't think I'd just casually toss out the babies line and hope that did it for you, eh?"

More laughing and crying at the same time. Beth had a feeling that was going to be the rest of her life. "It really did it for me, I gotta tell you."

"Mmm, I can't wait to find out just how wet that made you."

"Finn!" She gasped.

"What? Is there a rule that proposals can't have a bit of dirty talk in them? I'll edit this part out when we tell people how this went down."

"You better," she whispered.

"Beth Stewart, you are the most delicious woman I've ever met. You drive me mental and push all of my buttons, and there's no one else I'd rather go to sleep on a couch with. Or in a bed, or even a tent if you insisted. You push me to remember my soul and in doing so you renew my faith in humanity. You're kind and hard-working and really, truly beautiful. I'm particularly fond of your legs. And I'd like to wake up tangled in them every morning for the rest of my life. Will you do me the great honour of becoming my wife?"

"Yes. Yes, yes, yes. A million times yes." She closed the gap and pulled him up to stand over her as she slid on the ring.

He lifted her fingers to his mouth and pressed an open kiss to each of her knuckles. "There are some things in life we can plan for. And there are others that just need to be a leap of faith. I wasn't planning on falling in love with you, Beth. But I did. And it happened a long time ago. I've wasted enough time being pig-headed. How quickly can you plan a wedding?"

She wrapped her arms around his neck and pulled his mouth to hers. After kissing her fiancé senseless, she turned and led him upstairs to her bedroom, dropping her dress in the hallway.

EPILOGUE

Three months later

"That's my girl."

Beth woke up on her wedding day with Finn's voice in her ear and his cock sliding between her thighs. The perfect wake up. She arched her back, welcoming him into her body. "Do we have time?"

"We'll make time." He snaked his arms around her, pressing one into her belly and cupping a breast in the other. "Morning seems like the only time you're interested now, so I'll take what I can get."

She was just six weeks pregnant, but fatigue had already hit her. It was a blessing they were having a luncheon reception because there was no way she'd be up for a late night of dancing. "It's just the first trimester. That'll pass."

"I'm not complaining. I love morning sex." He groaned as she swivelled her hips. "Do you think you can come like this?"

"If you use your fingers."

"Tell me," he panted as he picked up the pace. She grinned but he bit her earlobe. "Be a good girl and tell me what you want. Tell me how you want me to get you off. Tell me how. You. Want. To. Come."

Each of his words worked just as well as a lick of his tongue or a stroke of his finger and he knew it. She moaned and arched even further, trying to angle her pelvis into the fingers that were teasing the hair on her sex. "Rub my clit…between two fingers."

He did exactly as she asked, exactly as she liked. They'd learned so much about each other over the last three months, and not just in the bedroom. He'd moved into her townhouse and one of her kitchen drawers suddenly turned into a catch-all junk space. The neat freak had a dirty secret. And Finn discovered that she really wasn't a morning person but she woke up at six to spend thirty minutes on the treadmill anyway. It didn't take much to convince her to try alternate ways of burning off some calories at dawn. She switched her treadmill time to the evening when he'd spend at least an hour working after dinner.

"You're thinking too much, gorgeous." He pinched her nipple. "Focus or I'll bite your neck."

"Thoughts of you, I promise," she gasped. "And you wouldn't! My dress is strapless."

"You don't think I'd mark you?" His dark words did their job and she started to clench around him. He kept up his steady strum at the top of her cleft as he surged in and out. "That's it. Come on me. Come for me. Come—"

And she did, exploding in his arms like a confetti cannon of joy. He followed with his own release, and thirty seconds later their alarm clock went off.

They laughed and kissed, sharing a happy, sweaty embrace, then they scrambled, each trying to get the shower first because it really wasn't big enough for them both. Finn hated her small en suite bathroom—it was the only part of his condo that he missed, and she couldn't deny him that one change. So while they were away on their honeymoon, the wall between the en suite and the next room over would be knocked down and both rooms renovated. They'd end up with a much larger bathroom with his and her sinks and an oversized shower. The former bedroom on the other side would lose its closet and some floor space but the new space would be just big enough for Finn's home office.

Eventually they'd need to move but the townhouse would be big enough for them and one child. As Beth brushed her teeth and watched Finn soap up quickly, she smoothed her hand over her lower belly. Still just a bundle of cells but she couldn't help but feel like one might be enough. She couldn't imagine feeling more complete or happier than she did at that moment.

— —

Finn's family showed up an hour later with a couple bottles of champagne, croissants and a fruit tray. Next arrived Beth's parents, who'd flown in for the wedding, then a make-up artist and a hairdresser. All the women disappeared upstairs and a few minutes later his mother fluttered downstairs carrying his suit bag.

"You should get dressed down here," she instructed. It made her anxious enough that Finn would see Beth before the ceremony. He decided not to torture her by sharing that not only had he already seen Beth's dress, he'd seen the lingerie she was wearing underneath it and they'd taken the entire outfit for a bit of a test-run, a memory which gave him a bit of a hard-on even in mixed company. It would be wrong to give his mother a heart attack on one of the happiest days of her life.

And his. He couldn't keep a grin off his face.

Not once in the last three months had he regretted leaping into a life with Beth. She got him, without judgement or complaint, except for when he packed up dinner leftovers when she'd secretly wanted seconds. And even then, when he packed those leftovers into a lunch bag for her the next day, he got a heated kiss as thanks, so she obviously didn't mind that much.

He stepped into the powder room on the main floor and changed into his suit, but his dress socks were upstairs in his dresser. He jogged halfway up the stairs and called out for Beth.

Giggles ensued and then her voice rang out. "Yes, darling?"

Fuck, he liked hearing her say that. "My socks."

"Hang on."

And he did, like a love-struck goofball, waiting for his wife-to-be to toss his socks over the bannister. When she did, he saw a glimpse of tulle and his breath caught in his throat. She hadn't worn a veil when she'd modelled her dress for him.

"Hey, Finn?" Her voice floated down to him. "How about you guys go on ahead to the winery and we'll meet you there?"

"You sure?"

He could hear the smile in her voice. "Absolutely."

The photographer was arriving as they left, and she took a few pictures of him and his brother, then the two of them with their dad. His mom came outside to press a boutonnière onto his lapel, and the photographer's assistant quietly appeared with a corsage for Finn to put on his mom's wrist. She cried, they took another picture, and then they escaped into the car. Ryan's son came racing out of the house at the last minute, so they needed to pause to move a booster seat from one car to the other, and Finn didn't mind even for a second.

At the winery, Evan and Ty were playing host, greeting guests at the front doors. Fall had arrived in Wardham and the decorations inside reflected that with colourful leaves and cranberries everywhere. They'd hired an external catering company to provide lunch and do event management but the West brothers were perfectionists and had taken special care to make their space special for Beth. Finn shook their hands, thanked them again, and when Ryan passed over his flask, shared a quick toast to his bride.

Finn had always enjoyed weddings—for the bridesmaids, usually, but also the casual elegance and slow pace of an entire day of celebration—but his own seemed to proceed at warp speed. Before he knew it, he was standing at the top of an aisle in the foyer. They'd only invited seventy-five people, so the ceremony was in the modern double story space and lunch would be served in the great hall. He expected Beth to come in the double doors and walk down the aisle, past their seated guests, but after her mother walked in and sat down, the justice of the peace instead pointed to the second story. The music changed, everyone rose, and out from her office stepped Beth with her father, a veil hanging down her back, framing her face.

Finn started laughing, which most people wouldn't understand, but Beth did. A gorgeous, wide smile cut across her face as she realized he appreciated her surprise. As they slowly stepped down the staircase, his heart rate sped up.

Her father kissed her at the bottom of the stairs then joined his wife in the front row. Beth held her hands out and Finn took them.

"You're shaking," she whispered.

"I don't get married every day." He blew out a long breath. "Ready?"

"Oh yeah. You ready?"

"I've been ready for months, my girl."

— —

The vows, a reading by Finn's sisters, the exchange of rings and signing of the registry all swam by in a haze. Beth had been warned by many of her friends that she might not be able to take it all in, and she was glad she'd hired a videographer. She wondered how many times she'd touch her tummy in the video, and giggled at their secret news. She'd taken a random server from the catering company into her confidence and the young girl brought her custom poured flutes of ginger ale and club soda that looked just like champagne.

They had their first dance before lunch, and at the end Finn gave a repeat performance of the big dip and halfway indecent kiss he'd planted on her at the end of the ceremony. Then it was time for feasting, although Beth wanted to sit and visit with everyone so while the others visited the buffet and tucked in, she circled the tables and thanked everyone for coming. She posed for pictures until her cheeks hurt from smiling, and when Finn wrapped his big hand around the outside curve of her waist and pointed her to their seats, she wanted to protest.

"You need to eat, my wife," he said, brushing his lips against her ear, his voice low and for her alone. "Feed my baby."

So she sat and tucked into the plate of food her husband brought her.

THE END

ACKNOWLEDGMENTS
aka The People Who Remind Me I'm Stronger than I Think

FIRST thank yous need to go out to my street team, the Wardham Ambassadors. These amazing fans cheered me on as I wrote Beth and Finn, promised me they would love it when it was done and then they did, even though they read an early version that was riddled with comma splices and repetitive words. Aarati, Allison, Amber, Andrea, Bette, Carole, Christine, Denise, Holly, Joy, Karn, Keri, Kim, LaLani, Lori, Maria, Marlene, Melissa, Mona, Pamela, Rachel, Shari, Shelly, Tina, and all the other fans who've joined the reader group over the last six months, you seriously make my day when I log in to Facebook. Special thanks Shelly and Marlene who caught typos and missing words, and Mona for her tireless dedication to keeping me inspired with photos! And Carole, for finishing it first. There are sixty-eight reasons this book is dedicated to this group.

I also owe Anne Marsh, Molly McLain and Cora Seton huge thanks for their support and guidance as critique partners. Writing is a lonely process and it's amazing to have found such supportive friends who bring that perfect mix of getting what I'm trying to do and not being afraid to tell me when I'm missing the mark. And reminding me, with endless patience, that crutch words and comma splices do not a good book make. If you haven't read their books yet, make that a priority for your to-read pile. They're all better writers than me, you're in for a treat. (See what I did there? Anne did. She's laughing.)

On the home front, I always need to give a nod to The Viking (aka my husband) for nodding and smiling and supporting me no matter what. The little Vikings, too, especially the 6 year old who has finally wrapped his head around the fact that by "making books" his mommy isn't actually doing the printing and binding, and that's okay. My in-laws, who feed my kids dinner while I type away in their living room. My friends and my sister and brother-in-law, who know that all conversations will eventually end up in Wardham. More nodding, more smiling. I love you all for putting up with me. Thank you.

My sister also humoured me as I called her up in the middle of the night (also known as just after the eleven o'clock news) with marketing questions. For that she gets her own line in the acknowledgements this time around. Panda rocks!

And last but not least, all the readers from far and wide who have fallen in love with this little Canadian town. Thank you for loving Laney, Kyle, Carrie, Ian, Karen, Paul, Evie, Liam, all of their kids, and now Beth and Finn.

ABOUT THE AUTHOR

Zoe York lives in London, Ontario with her young family. She's currently chugging Americanos, wiping sticky fingers, and dreaming of heroes in and out of uniform.

www.zoeyork.com

28621718R00070

Printed in Great Britain
by Amazon